THE SKY UNWASHED

THE SKY UNWASHED

A NOVEL

IRENE ZABYTKO

ALGONQUIN BOOKS
OF CHAPEL HILL
2000

Published by
Algonquin Books of Chapel Hill
Post Office Box 2225
Chapel Hill, North Carolina 27515-2225

a division of Workman Publishing
708 Broadway, New York, New York 10003

A portion of Chapter II was previously published in altered form
in *Earth Tones: Creative Perspectives on Ecological Issues*,
edited by Belinda Subraman, Vergin Press, El Paso, Texas, 1994
as "Matushka's Arrival."

Library of Congress Cataloging-in-Publication Data

Zabytko, Irene.
    The sky unwashed : a novel / by Irene Zabytko.
      p.   cm.
    ISBN 1-56512-246-1 (hardcover)
    1. Chernobyl Nuclear Accident, Chornobyl§' Ukraine, 1986—
Fiction. 2. Aged women—Ukraine—Fiction. 3. Family—
Ukraine—Fiction. I. Title.
PS3576.A167 S58   2000
813'.54—dc21   99-053476

10 9 8 7 6 5 4 3 2 1
First Edition

For my mother, Maria Zabytko, and in memory

of my father, Ostap Stanley Zabytko

And in memory of the "thirty-one"

THE SKY UNWASHED

And the sky is unwashed, and the waves are sleepy,
And beyond the shore, far, far away,
The reeds, as though drunk,
Sway without wind. Merciful Lord!
How much longer do I have
In this open prison,
This useless sea,
This tedious world? It doesn't speak.
Silent and bent as if alive,
The steppes' yellowed grasses
Won't tell the truth.
And there's no one else to ask.

—Taras Shevchenko, 1848

(Translated from the Ukrainian by Irene Zabytko.)

CHORNOBYL: WORMWOOD *(Artemisia vulgaris)*

   . . . and there fell a great star from heaven,
burning as it were a lamp, and it fell upon the third
part of the rivers, and upon the fountains of waters;
   . . . And the name of the star is called Wormwood:
and the third part of the waters became wormwood;
and many men died of the waters, because they
were made bitter . . . (Revelation 8:10–11)

AUTHOR'S NOTE

When an author writes in one alphabet and her characters speak in another, the problem of transliteration arises. Because the characters in this book speak in Ukrainian and at times in Russian, I have used the English transliterations from both these languages (*e.g.,* Kyiv and Kiev, Chornobyl and Chernobyl, etc.).

THE SKY UNWASHED

PROLOGUE

In the village of Starylis, during the less politically oppressive days of the Gorbachev era in the Soviet Union, the citizens working on the *kolhosp,* the collective farm, felt themselves to be more prosperous than their counterparts in the cities of Ukraine. The cows' milk was sweet and creamy because the animals were allowed to roam the fertile grasslands. From a distance, fleshy black cows dotted the crisp hay fields where they ate the tender and abundant lemongrass and clover. Near the fields, wild red-orange poppies grew defiantly between the giant stalks of sunflowers.

Old men chewed tobacco and sunflower seeds during harvest time so as not to set fire to the dry igloo-shaped bundles of hay with their homemade cigarettes, while the strong, overworked women tended the cows and ran the tractors alongside their men. When they weren't too busy with the farmwork, the women still made traditional jam from Queen Anne's lace, a golden paste they spread on generous slices of soft brown breads often baked in the huge outdoor clay ovens their ancestors had fired for over a hundred years.

The old men and women were clearly in charge of the *kolhosp*. Because of the stubbornness they inherited from their serf forbears, they insisted on harboring pieces of the land for their own small gardens. The government reluctantly allowed each of them one-third of an acre of property. So the villagers' thatched-roofed houses stood on these modest patches of cleared forest land, surrounded by neat gardens of potatoes, beets, tomatoes and pretty ornamental flowers that the older women grew to adorn the altar in the church. A few families even managed to build tiny sheds on the corners of their crowded lots, which they used to smoke pork, or to hide a still, or to shelter a cow. In the fall, the old women gathered huge, succulent white mushrooms and strung and dried the feathery caps into amber curls that would sell to the highest or loudest bidder on Saturday mornings at the local bazaars.

But the old farmers' children weren't so stubborn. They preferred to seek the better wages at the nuclear power plant in nearby Chornobyl. There, the gray cement modern buildings were a monument to the Soviet promise of progress. Everyone knew that if you could last five years doing whatever work they gave you, you were eligible to apply for a short family vacation at the plant's residence in the resort town of Sochi on the Black Sea. Ten years on the job got you a booklet of coupons that permitted you to shop at the *kashtan,* the stores that were only for tourists with hard currency or for Communist Party officials. At the *kashtan,* you could buy transistor radios and mock oriental rugs. Sometimes, sexy ivory nylon blouses from East Germany or ice-pink lipsticks from Poland would come in unexpectedly and be bought up in minutes, before the next surprise product appeared without warning on the shelves.

Until their names came up on the interminable waiting lists for the ever-crowded, dour blocks of Stalinesque apartments closest to the Chornobyl plant, this new generation lived in Starylis with their parents and grandparents. Together, the generations mingled, fought and survived in the cramped village cottages because, for the meantime, they had no place else to go. They rebuilt the roofs, especially the thatched ones which always needed repair after a hard winter, or pooled their monthly wages to buy a new cow or a new kind of television without the horizontal lines that defaced the screen whenever anyone was trying to watch a news program or a rock concert direct from Moscow. The more affluent families of Starylis could even afford a car, a Volga or Lada usually, black and sturdy, complete with a diesel engine that could blow the dust on the country roads even further than a tractor could.

What the younger villagers of Starylis wanted most was to bring some material comfort into their hard, barren lives. Years of empty Communist promises had led to apathy and disillusionment and made them hunger for the tangible possessions they thought would soothe their frustrated spirits.

For their part, the older generation—the ones who had survived Stalin, famine and war, especially the *babysi,* the old women in babushkas who kept the old ways alive with their icons and litanies despite the official ban on religion—knew that the hard times never end.

In 1986, Paraskevia Volodymyrivna told the other *babysi* of Starylis that the storks had not returned to nest on her thatched roof. This had happened only twice before during her lifetime—in 1933 at the height of Stalin's artificial famine and in 1944 when the Germans invaded the village. A bad sign, Paraskevia told anyone passing her house who would listen. Maybe they'll come yet, many said to appease the old woman. But Paraskevia shook her head. The storks had always returned just when the long thick icicles under the eaves melted and dripped like a death knoll to announce the end of winter. By the time the first crocuses opened their sassy yellow petals, and the buds on the naked trees were about to green and swell, the storks should already have been settled into their wide nests.

A bad sign, Paraskevia repeated to herself. She made the sign of the cross and expected something to happen.

PART I

Back in a Few Days . . .

Chapter 1

MARUSIA PETRENKO'S HANDS were coarse and red, thickened over the years by hard work, bad weather and indifference, and yet the pads on the tips of her fingers were as soft as a baby's bald crown. Her hands were numb to most sensations and especially to the hot water she poured over the socks of her only son Yurko—a man in his forties, and she in her seventies. The washing of his socks and underwear was a habit Marusia chose to keep even though Yurko had a wife.

She used the yellow lye soap from the Starylis co-op store that was used in all the homes in the village. It was locally made by the old men, and they could never agree on how much lanolin to put in, nor had they the creative bent to dash in some essence of violets to make a more luxurious and feminine soap for the ladies—the men simply didn't care about such things. Marusia rubbed the thick cake hard against the material and sloshed the socks in the little copper sink. The underwear and socks, heavy with water, were wrung through her long fingers, the water scalding her knuckles. She furiously fought the stains and throttled the cheap, thinning fabrics with the blows of her powerful hands—turning, splashing, until the front of her dress became soaked with a vest of wetness over her ample breasts.

Next she would wash her grandchildren's things—little Katia's socks with the pink lace on the cuffs that came from Czechoslovakia, and Tarasyk's cloth diapers. He was still in diapers at three, but Marusia didn't mind. He was a happy child who hummed to himself though he hardly ever spoke because, Marusia thought, his parents argued constantly and muted the stuttering sounds of his sweet baby voice.

On the nights when she wasn't too angry at her daughter-in-law, she would also wash Zosia's laundry, although Zosia seemed to expect it rather than be grateful. Lately, Zosia appeared more impudent than usual, stomping around in her new red and yellow vinyl-strapped high heels. Unlike many of the Slavic girls in the village, Zosia's calves and thighs were straight and narrow and not thick and solid like tree stumps. "Those must be new shoes, they look so modern," Marusia said to her the first time Zosia wriggled her feet into them. Zosia mumbled offhandedly that her mother had sent the shoes to her as a gift all the way from Siberia where she lived. Marusia clamped shut her mouth, even though she assumed that the shoes were a gift from one of the men friends Zosia whored around with.

Marusia never openly accused Zosia of being unfaithful to Yurko; there was no point in provoking Zosia's bad temper. Above all, the children had to be protected from their parents' silly problems. It'll work itself out, she hoped, pursing her lips as she threw the heavy, wet clothes around in the sink. "*Bozhe,* what a *hom,*" she said to herself. "For a pair of shoes that one would spread her legs for the devil."

On this particular evening, Marusia listened to the television on in the next room as she washed. An announcer was narrating a travelogue on Tbilisi in the Russian language. Marusia had never been to any large Soviet city. Anything she learned about the Soviet Union or the world came from watching the television. She avoided the talk programs (too political for her tastes), but she loved to watch the travelogues. Once she neglected making dinner because she was enraptured by a documentary on the alligators in America, in a place called *Floridoo.* "Teeth the size of a horseradish root," she'd tell anyone who would listen. "And a tail that could knock you off your feet in a second," she'd say proudly, as if the alligators belonged to her.

Marusia went into the living room to watch the end of the program on Tbilisi. She wanted to ask Yurko a question about Georgia, where people lived to be over a hundred years old God bless them, and to ask him was it true that the dark Georgian men, who drank so much wine, were good to their wives and to old people. She had heard rumors that they were not wife beaters, but the television programs would never report about things like that. Yurko, however, was sprawled out on the divan, snoring, a half-empty glass of warm brown beer on the floor near his stockinged feet. She gently kissed his head, which rested on one of her own pillows that she had elaborately cross-stitched in red and black poppies. At first, she wanted to take it from beneath his greasy hair—such little wisps of thin brown threads that hardly covered his premature baldness. But she felt sorry for him and decided to let him sleep.

He works so hard, she thought to herself. Lately, he had been logging overtime hours at the Chornobyl plant, where he did something with electricity—what, she wasn't sure, since he hardly ever talked to her about his work—it all seemed so mysterious and so important. He did explain that he wanted to put in more time, so that he would be considered for a promotion and sent to a special school where the plant's engineers were trained.

Marusia noticed that his undershirt was stained with sweat, and she wished she had asked for it before he fell asleep.

She stooped to stroke her son's hair, but Bosyi, the German shepherd asleep on the floor, awoke and growled.

"Sh, I won't wake him," she said with a smile. Bosyi thumped his tail and whined as though he were apologizing in advance for intervening in case she bothered his master. "See, I'm going," she whispered, and returned to the kitchen to resume her washing.

The water had turned blue from the cheap dye of the socks. She opened the drain stopper and watched the water gurgle slowly down the drain before she twisted and rinsed out the wet bundles. Marusia hung the clothing on the pegs fastened to the ceiling beams directly above the large tiled cookstove, where the dripping water caused a steady hissing on the cast-iron lids.

As Marusia was hanging up the clothes, Zosia came into the kitchen in her thin cotton robe which only half concealed her lacy black bra and slip. She drank milk straight out of the glass bottle and ignored Myrrko, the gray cat, who appeared out of the shadows to rub herself against Zosia's firm legs.

"*Bozhe,*" Marusia whispered, eyeing her. "You're going to have another?"

Zosia quickly wiped her mouth with her sleeve. "What about it?" she said defiantly. "Anyway, I'm not sure I want it." She poured the milk into a dish for the cat. "Here sweetie, have the rest."

Zosia was still a good-looking woman at twenty-eight, with classic high cheekbones that sculpted the otherwise flat planes of her face. She was shapely and slender, with a matronly softness settling into her hips and waist. Her dark blue eyes were duller than the turquoise luster they'd had when she was a girl, but could still radiate great warmth whenever she smiled, which wasn't often. She would have been prettier without the stiff blond hair that she kept teased up into an unflattering beehive with the tattered ends tucked severely behind her ears. Her natural color was a softer, quieter chestnut, but she chose a shade of blond that became more brittle with each monthly dye treatment she received at the beauty shop near the Chornobyl plant.

Zosia pulled her robe around her stomach. "Don't worry—it's easier for me to keep this one than to get rid of it." Because abortion was the only available birth control in the Soviet Union, Zosia had not mourned her four past abortions. She knew women who had had twelve or fifteen, and she expected as many for herself if she kept up her sexual lifestyle. Unfortunately, the last time she was at the abortion clinic, the anesthetic failed her, and she had screamed from the pain when they suctioned the tissue out of her. The nurses in their starched white coned hats and shifts had held her down and yelled at her to shut up, it was nothing, what a fuss she was making! Zosia had thought she was going to die.

She felt nauseated from the memory and blamed it on the rich creamy milk. "I'll probably keep this one, *Mamo*," she said.

"Thank God," sighed Marusia, who had herself miscarried three babies before Yurko was born. Marusia cleared her throat but would not ask if this child was really Yurko's. It doesn't matter, she sternly told herself. It was Yurko's as long as he was married to Zosia. That's how it had to be. She would coddle it and love it and teach it lessons, the sort that Yurko and Zosia did not approve of, like the chants for the Mass and knowing whether or not to fast before certain holy days.

"Don't tell him about it, not yet," Zosia said, nodding her head toward the other room. "I'll tell him later. When things are better." She clopped out of the kitchen to watch television. Marusia heard her changing the channels and turning the volume on louder, and then she heard the dog barking and Yurko's hoarse voice telling Zosia to turn it off and leave him alone.

"When will things get better?" the old woman asked the cat, who sat staring at her empty bowl, expecting more milk. "I haven't seen them get along for one complete day since they were married." She ran fresh water into the sink for the next load, turning the water taps on full blast so as to drown out Zosia's voice calling out to her son.

Chapter 2

WEDDINGS WERE A common occurrence in Starylis. So were divorces, but those weren't publicly celebrated as much except by the men in the community who got together to slander the women, and to drink the home-brewed hundred-proof *samohon* someone would always bring to offer the man who was set free.

Most of the marriage celebrations in the village were planned for the late spring, because the Soviet government encouraged the young people to openly defy the Lenten prohibition against weddings. The older people were too powerless to protest, and would go along with their grandchildren's weddings if they could somehow include some of the old traditions. Gradually, more weddings were performed in the Soviet city halls and in the churches which the Communists allowed to operate provided that a government-appointed priest officiated. The government's priest in Starylis was Father Andrei, who happened to work at the Chornobyl plant. He was glad enough for both jobs, and eager to perform any church wedding the KGB allowed him, regardless of the contradictory situation he and his flock had to endure.

Marusia could not remember a spring when she and her family had not attended many weddings. She decided that out of the several that would take place in the village over the coming weekend, she would attend the wedding of the granddaughter of Evdokia Zenoviivna. Evdokia had promised that the ceremony would be traditional and Christian, held in the village church and performed by the priest, and not the usual unholy service where the bride and groom simply signed a register at the ZAKS, the magistrate's office.

Evdokia had expressly asked Marusia to bake her famous wedding bread—a *korovai*—for the reception, a party that Evdokia declared would be special because her son-in-law, "that stupid Bolshevik," had been able to rent the *klub,* the village social center, for the occasion. The *klub* was also the village headquarters for the *komsomol* meetings, and everyone knew that because Evdokia's granddaughter and bride-to-be, Hanna Koval, was past *komsomol* president, and because her father had paid off the *klub*'s director, theirs was the only wedding party given permission to use the building that weekend. Since Evdokia had insisted Hanna get married in the church, Hanna balanced public opinion by having the rest of her ceremony—"the best part," as she put it—at the most obvious Communist building in the village.

Marusia spent all day Thursday preparing the dough for the huge *korovai* before carrying it to the communal outdoor oven a short walk down the dirt road from her home. She liked using the old-style oven better than her own stove that heated either too quickly or not at all. She sat down on one of the wooden benches and thought what a warm day it was, warmer than the past few weeks.

"*Slava Isusu Khrystu,*" said the reedy voice of Slavka Lazorska, who was making her way up the little hill to where Marusia sat. Slavka Lazorska held a jar of clear liquid.

"*Slava na viky,*" answered Marusia. "God give you peace and health."

"And you," said Slavka Lazorska. The tall, lean woman sat down beside Marusia. "I smell your famous work of art. Whose wedding is it for this time?"

"Hanna's."

Slavka Lazorska snorted. "Oh, her. That one. She has to get married you know."

"Yes, I know." Marusia shook her head. "Well, these young ones with their, you know, modern socialism and . . ." She bent toward her friend and whispered, "sex."

"At least we had the decency to blame our bad behavior on the war," said Slavka Lazorska. The old women laughed.

"Now, no one bothers to excuse themselves," said Marusia. "They just sew material enough for two white wedding dresses and there it is, for anyone to see."

"So true. The little whores." Slavka Lazorska laughed. "I'm going to attend that other one's wedding—you know, Ania Podilenko. The one with the fake red hair. Somehow she's related to me, I don't know how. Probably from some bastard's side of the family I'm not even sure of. Everyone's related to me all of sudden when they want a present."

"What are you getting her?"

Lazorska untied her green and black paisley babushka and wiped her face with it. Her lank iron-gray braids were coiled tightly like chain mail and wrapped around her head several times. "Well, she—that other one, Ania—is not like that rabbit, Hanna. Ania has a hard time getting a baby. So I made up an herbal potion to help her along. She's no young chicken, either. Way past thirty, and this her fourth marriage."

Marusia was impressed. Slavka Lazorska was the village healer, as all the women in her family had been. She boasted that she was never sick a day in her life, not even during the war when people dropped in the streets like acorns after a windstorm. Her garden was the largest patch of privately owned land in Starylis. In it, she grew all of the herbs and plants she used in her treatments. And she worked with the cups—large glass jars heated over a flame which she strategically applied to soothe the arthritis in a sore leg or loosen the phlegm in an inflamed chest. Lazorska was famous for her poultices and mustard plasters and was particularly revered for knowing the right cures for women's ailments, especially when a woman lost her female pleasure juices or the "gripping powers" in a womb that should cushion and hold a child inside.

Marusia was a little afraid of Lazorska and only called on her when prayers and conventional medicine failed.

She had first met Slavka Lazorska during the horrible typhus epidemic right after the war. The Red Cross had not gotten medical supplies through to Starylis. Marusia's mother was near death before she begged her daughter to fetch the "*dokhtor*," the title given to Slavka Lazorska's own mother. Marusia couldn't find her, but brought back the daughter, whose hair was coal black then, as were her arched eyebrows that met in the center of her high forehead, her skin taut and smooth as an olive. When Marusia first saw her, she felt sure she was a witch or a Gypsy and distrusted her exotic darkness. Even so, Slavka Lazorska cooled Marusia's old mother with a healing poultice mixed in snow that quenched her fever and resurrected her.

The second time Marusia called on Lazorska was when she was far along into her sad marriage and begged for an herb to conceive a child. "It might keep him at home," Marusia had confessed to Lazorska in shame. From it, Yurko her son was born, and Marusia always remembered that she owed the healer two more major, unrepayable debts—one for her son's birth, the other that Lazorska never betrayed Marusia's secret.

"Is that the gift?" Marusia asked shyly, pointing to the jar.

"This? Oh, no! This is just some vintage leftover *samohon* Fed'ko at the co-op wanted me to sample. Here, have a taste." She unscrewed the top of the jar and held the pure grain vodka out to Marusia.

"*Na zdorovia,*" Marusia said. She took a long swig. "Ahh. Thank you. Very good. *Luxe.* First class."

"Yes, it's about the best I've had all season. But he better not try to sell me any. You know, I gave that devil's son my own recipe. And then he has the nerve to tell me it's from an ancient family formula that was handed down from his great great great Kozak grandfather who slept with the tzarina's horse or some such cow shit."

The women laughed. Slavka Lazorska took her turn and wiped her mouth with the sleeve of her woolen cardigan before handing the jar back to Marusia. The healer smiled openly at her, exposing the gold in her teeth and brightening her sallow, triangular face.

Marusia's head felt light, and the sun's rays were warm and comforting on her face. She remembered a lullaby her mother had taught her a long time ago. Lazorska's voice was off key and lower than Marusia's, but she hummed along as she tried to pick up the melody. Marusia's eyes misted, and she blew her nose into a handkerchief she had tucked in her dress pocket.

"Sometimes, I miss my mother so much," she confessed, thinking that she would sing the song to her grandchildren later that night.

"She was a good woman," Slavka Lazorska said. "Bless her soul."

Marusia sighed and, measuring the sun's shadow on the grass beneath their feet, reckoned that she had had the bread in for about the right amount of time. She peeked into the clay oven and took the loaf out carefully with a long, flat wooden shovel.

"Oh, what beautiful bread," whispered Slavka Lazorska, as if the loaf might cave in if her voice were too loud.

Marusia placed the walnut-brown loaf on the picnic table. She was pleased. It was a magnificent *korovai,* a huge round braided bread decorated with several birds also made of dough, kissing one another. Later, when it cooled, she would place some sprigs of periwinkle and flowers among the birds.

"Yes, it turned out very well."

"I hope that silly little potato appreciates it," Lazorska said. She took her turn with the vodka.

"I don't care," Marusia said, gladly taking the offered jar. "As long as it's noticed as much as the bride's dress." She spotted a brown skylark flying in circles with a twig in its mouth. On a nearby branch, its mate stood chirping at him. The women watched.

"Look, she's telling him what to do," Slavka Lazorska pointed. The male flew back to his mate on the branch, who abruptly took the twig from out of his beak and flew alone to another tree. He followed her to a half-built nest well concealed in the cradle of the higher branches and humbly watched her entwine his meager donation within the delicate bowl of twigs and straw.

Slavka Lazorska laughed. "You see how it is! The females always have to do the work of the males! Even the male *birds* can't do anything by themselves, because they don't know how."

"That's the blessed truth!"

Then they sat in idle silence, breathing in the air and the scent of the fresh bread, listening to the low rumbles of a threshing machine in the distance.

Marusia made a small sign of the cross over the bread. "Well, anyway, thank God we've made it through another winter." She shooed away tiny flies lingering over her bread and covered it with a towel. "I wish I could offer you some of this bread."

"You make one for me for my wedding," teased Lazorska, who had buried five or so husbands and outlived several more lovers than she cared to admit she remembered.

Chapter 3

"I CAN'T HELP it if I have to work later tonight!"
Yurko had raised his voice at Zosia. It was Friday morning. Marusia was still in her bed, in the room she shared
with Tarasyk and Katia. Only a thin curtain separated it
from Zosia and Yurko's part of the house. The little boy,
Tarasyk, was still asleep, his thumb poised on his lower
lip. Marusia kissed his curls and brought the goose-down
coverlet closer to his chin. Katia was already up and in
the kitchen playing with the cat and dog before she was
sent off to school.

"You always have to work. You knew about the reception two weeks ago," Zosia shouted.

"How the hell can I remember something as stupid
as somebody's wedding two weeks ago."

"Yes, that's how you are. But six months ago you
made a date with your friends to go fishing, and you remember it like your own birthday."

"What the hell are you talking about? I didn't have any date to go fishing. The weather just turned to spring a few damn days ago. . . ."

"Right. So like a thief in a palace, off you'll go next weekend with your drunken, rotten friends on a boat . . . that you'll do. But when I want to go somewhere, where there's a wedding and dancing, and people, you have to work. . . ."

"All right, I'll go to the damn wedding. I'll go to the stupid reception. But I have to leave by nine-thirty for the night shift. You can stay all night and dance with every goddamn fool and his brother 'til your big feet swell like rockets, and you can do whatever the devil else you want to do. I don't give a good goddamn. . . ."

"*Oy, yoy, yoy,*" Marusia grumbled out loud so that they would hear her. They can't go a day without fighting about something stupid, she thought.

Marusia didn't like to overhear their arguments, but the house was small, only three and a half rooms, built in a circle with the kitchen in the center. Zosia and Yurko's room was so close to hers that it was hard to ignore the sounds of suppressed rage and anger or of the sporadic lovemaking that in their earlier years together used to always follow their battles. Zosia was usually the more emotional and dramatic of the two, sometimes —when she felt especially wounded or when he ignored her—adding to the venom of her voice by throwing things at Yurko. Yurko was more controlled perhaps only because he was so much older than she. Marusia had been relieved when her son finally married at the elderly age of thirty-five, although, when she first laid eyes on the young Zosia, surly and demanding even then, with her thick makeup and wild yellow hair, she thought to herself, What a *prostytutka*.

Zosia and Yurko met working together at the electronics section of the nuclear power plant. Yurko was Zosia's supervisor, and they had become lovers on the long lonely nights when they should have been preoccupied with the instruments on the generators that connected to the turbines of the nuclear reactors. They married when Zosia was pregnant with Katia.

Marusia crawled out of the bed and stiffly put on her sweater over her flannel nightgown. "Good, they stopped," she said to herself. She knelt on the cold hardwood floor and said her morning prayers, praying especially for Zosia to mend her mean ways and be more *myla*—quieter and kinder—to Yurko.

Katia skipped into the room. "I fed Myrrko." Katia giggled. "I gave him all your beautiful bread."

"Oh you naughty one," Marusia said, pinning the little honey-haired girl against her and kissing her head. "Would you like some breakfast yourself?"

"Yes." Katia began to brush Marusia's unplaited, wavy gray hair. "*Babo?* I didn't really give Myrrko your bread. Just a mouse."

"Much better, but I was saving that mouse for your dinner, *dorohen'ka*," Marusia said. They both giggled loud enough to awake Tarasyk, who was rubbing his eyes.

"Wake up darling, the birds are singing, the sun is shining," Marusia sang to Tarasyk, who smiled. It was the same song she always sang for the children in the mornings.

IN THE KITCHEN, Marusia was surprised to find Zosia ironing a dress shirt for Yurko. "So, good morning," Marusia said. Yurko sat at the veneered wooden table in his T-shirt and his best navy blue striped trousers, drinking his black tea from a tall glass and eating leftover potatoes and sour cream. His rounded shoulders were stooped from worry, and his face was more haggard-looking from the new growth of heavy beard sprinkling his chin.

"So, *sonechko*, you and Zosia are going to the wedding?" she asked, trying to sound casual.

"Well, Mama, it's hard to keep anything from you," Yurko said, slumping further into his chair.

"A regular *Cheka* agent," Zosia said, and suppressed a short laugh.

Marusia pursed her lips and ignored them. She turned her attention to preparing kasha for the children. Katia was helping her brother wash at the sink. Bosyi the dog was at his usual place, beneath the table at Yurko's slippered feet, his tail thumping happily whenever he felt Yurko's leg twitch. Except to the children, Marusia did not speak again until Zosia noticed the *korovai* in the larder when she went to fetch some powdered cornstarch which she used to stiffen Yurko's shirt collar and cuffs. "Oh! *Mamo,*" she yelled. "It's beautiful! The best one you ever made! Yurko, come in and take a look."

Yurko got up and went grudgingly into the larder. "Beautiful, *Mamo!*" he echoed.

"It looks just like a soft cloud," said Katia.

IN APRIL OF that particular year, the days were unseasonably warm and mild. The dirt roads leading around the village were muddy because the ground had thawed too quickly from the recent hard frosts.

The morning of Hanna's wedding was especially tranquil except for a few billowing clouds that had at first threatened rain, but released only a quick, clean shower before the sun reappeared in all its warm brilliance. Marusia made her way to Evdokia's home, where a large group of villagers was waiting outside in the garden for Hanna and her groom to arrive. These older villagers and some of Hanna's friends had gathered to see the *blahoslovennia,* the traditional blessings given by the elders in the bride's family on her wedding day. Evdokia Zenoviivna and her husband, Oleh the beekeeper, sat stoically on wooden slat chairs in front of their tidy white-washed house. They wore traditional Ukrainian folk costumes: Evdokia in her long red skirt, embroidered sash and blouse; her husband in his own embroidered shirt and long red sash that wound several times around his narrow waist, and which also held up a pair of satin blue *sharavary,* the balloon-wide pants that had fit him more snugly in his younger days.

"We're taking bets to see if Hanna and the drunk she's marrying will show up," Marusia overheard the man in front of her say.

"Oh, she'll come all right," said the stout woman next to him. "The grandparents promised Hanna her ruby necklaces and a wad of money Evdokia got from selling her cow. That'll help her get through the next winter, for sure, and now with a new little soul on the way . . ."

The crowd hushed one another and nodded their heads in the direction of a short woman, dressed in a long white wedding dress and veil, slowly making her way on the muddy road toward the crowd. The hem of her dress was dotted with wet mud, and her long veil dragged over the ground. She held a fading bouquet of pansies and tulips and hesitated each time her spiked heels caught in the mud. *"Do bisa!"* she cursed loudly when she nearly slipped and fell. She regained her balance and continued.

"Pick up the train of your dress," a woman in lavender lace shouted. "Or it will get dirty!"

"It's too late for that, Mama!" shouted the bride.

"Where's the groom?" someone snickered.

A robust young man, blond with watery blue eyes, and in workclothes from the Chornobyl plant, put down his lunch pail and ran toward the bride. He picked her up and carried her the rest of the way to the grandparents.

The crowd applauded. "Well done, Maksym,"

shouted the bride's father dressed in a blue pin-striped suit with a pink boutonniere.

"Maksym, you should marry her yourself," someone in the crowd shouted.

"And make my wife mad? No thank you!" Maksym said. The crowd laughed at the blushing man. Everyone knew what a bad-tempered woman he was married to.

"Good people, this is a solemn occasion," shouted the bride's mother. "Hanna go ahead." She gently pushed her daughter toward a tiny fringed rug beneath the grandparents' feet. Hanna knelt before them and grabbed their withered hands into her own. "Bless me *Babo* and *Didy*. I am about to leave my home and become a bride."

Some of the younger people were snickering. Hanna immediately recognized them as her friends from her job at the plant. "Hey Hanna, where's the groom? Maybe he went to the wrong wedding," yelled out a brassy-haired young woman with the same shade of lipstick as Hanna's.

Hanna stood up and turned around, shaking her bouquet at them. "You all just shut up or don't bother coming to the party later on!"

"Hanna, you shut up," her mother said. "Don't disrespect your grandparents. *Tatu,* wake up." She gently nudged her old father's shoulder.

"Oleh, wake up and speak to her," said Evdokia.

The old man looked up. His mustache was long and white, with dabs of beeswax turning up the corners, and he pulled on it as he spoke. "Well, nice to see everyone. Let's go to the church now. Come on. It won't kill you." He stood up and would have left, but his daughter grabbed him and firmly pressed his shoulders, leveling him back into his chair.

"Sit down, crazy fool," Evdokia whispered. "We can't go anywhere without the groom." She sighed. "Get up Hanna, no use waiting for your husband like that. You'll be on your knees long enough, you'll see, either praying over or cleaning up after that . . . that bad one." She shook her head. "You'll see."

"Hanna! Hanna!" A young man standing in a cart pulled by a white horse shouted in the distance. His light brown hair was darkened by hair cream, and he was dressed in a suit and a wide crimson tie that could have flagged any bull in a field. It was Ihor, Hanna's groom. He waved his hand, and a long, scandalous purple and green Italian silk scarf tied to his wrist flapped in the breeze. The three other men in the cart with him had similar scarves tied to their wrists rather than the traditional embroidered ones. One man quickly passed a bottle to the others, and each took a hefty swig before they came nearer to the old people's house. "Please, good people of God," the groom mumbled with a cigarette dangling from the corner of his full mouth. "Please, good people of God . . . please come to the wedding."

"Yes, come to the wedding," chortled his friends in the cart, waving to the crowd.

The white horse was old and having difficulty because the men kept taking turns at the reins. The crowd quickly separated when the squeaky wooden cart approached. Several men in the crowd had to hold the horse and calm it because it did not want to stop.

"Look out! Even the horse is drunk," a man shouted, and everyone laughed.

"Hanna, beloved, I came. See, I didn't forget," said Ihor.

Hanna placed her hand on her hip. "Fine, fine. I guess I should count myself very lucky. But as you probably don't know, it is our tradition to have the reception *after* the wedding."

"And the honeymoon after the wedding too," one of Hanna's girlfriends shouted. The crowd laughed. Hanna turned and stared into the group until she recognized the traitor. "You shut up, Masha. Just because you can't hold on to a man . . ."

Evdokia's short, stocky body appeared at her granddaughter's side. The old woman's apple cheeks were ruddier than usual, and her pug nose twitched like a rabbit's. "Stop it. You can't fight now, not in that dress or in your condition. Get on with the ceremony. You there, Ihor. Help her into the cart!"

Ihor hopped out unsteadily. He grabbed Evdokia's hand and kissed it. "Bless me, *Babo*. . . ."

Evdokia wrung her hand away from his grasp. "Stop that, you idiot! Get Hanna in the cart. The priest is waiting."

"You couldn't wait until later to get drunk?" Hanna hissed at Ihor as he and his friends strained to lift her in.

"Look, I might have changed my mind. . . ."

"You do, and I'll see that you never drink another thing in your life again because you'll be dead!"

"Oh my little Hanna, so heavy," Ihor said, dragging her up.

"Thanks to you!"

The men in the cart laughed and handed her the bottle.

"Go to hell," she whispered to them. Then she smiled at Ihor and pulled some hay from his hair. "What's this? Where did you sleep last night?"

"Your grandmother made me sleep in the barn—with the stinky pigs. They wanted to keep you pure. Of course, as a gentleman, I had to oblige. . . ."

She laughed and gently brushed the hay off his mustache. *"Koo-koo,"* she said in a small, high voice.

"Koo-koo-ri-koo," he replied in his loud rooster voice. They both giggled and bumped their foreheads together. The men in the cart guffawed and whistled with their fingers, and the crowd applauded.

Ihor tried to kiss her, but she turned her head. "Not now, wait a little bit longer." She turned to her audience and shouted, "Please come to the wedding good people of God."

The crowd cheered and walked behind the wedding party on the path that led directly to the wooden church at the other end of the village.

THE TINNY CHURCH bells rang. Inside the ancient —some said it was built in the seventeenth century— wooden building, the priest patiently waited for the observers to find a place to stand on the floor, since there were no pews. Ihor's friends made a path through the crowd to the altar. Hanna and Ihor shyly approached the priest standing before the iconostasis. Father Andrei was a young man whose hobnailed work boots, polished for the service, peeked out from beneath his gold brocade vestments. When he wasn't conducting services, he was a janitor at the Chornobyl plant. He lived with his mother, Paraskevia Volodymyrivna, who never missed a service her son was ministering, even this one, although she had carried a grudge against Evdokia and her family for over a decade. It had something to do with a sick chicken, but no one remembered the details.

Father Andrei looked stern beneath his mop of black karakul hair and behind his full beard. He cleared his throat and began the service once the bride and groom stood on the *rushnyk,* the embroidered linen wedding cloth. It was no secret that Hanna had hardly ever attended Mass, but she knew the exact moment when she was to walk in a circle three times. Then, both the bride and groom held lit candles that dripped hot beeswax on their hands as they waited for the priest to place the golden crowns on their heads, say the prayers, and then switch their crowns. Ihor and Hanna exchanged rings, and Ihor fumbled with the long silk scarf that was attached to his wrist before winding it around Hanna's hand so that it was bound together with his own.

"In the sight of God, I pronounce Ihor Hryhorich Bupko married to Hanna, his wife."

The wedding party congregated outside the church, and everyone wished the bride and groom great happiness. When a battered old black Volga drove up and honked, Ihor and Hanna waved to the crowds and piled into the backseat that was covered with fake leopard skins. They were going to the village center, where Hanna would place her bouquet on the war monument, a new custom practiced throughout the Soviet Union after the Great Patriotic War. Hanna's parents and several of the younger villagers followed the bride and groom. The older generation, including Evdokia and Oleh, refused to go and watch. "It's their tradition, not ours," Evdokia said, and the old men and women nodded.

THE *KLUB,* A fairly large building, was packed full with guests, some invited and others not. Vodka, made by Hanna's father from the best potatoes harvested from his own garden, flowed out of barrels. But the bride and groom were toasted first with champagne and then with grandfather Oleh's bottle of mead, which his feisty bees had helped produce two seasons earlier. He poured the syrupy golden liquid into two shot glasses, one for himself and one for the bride and groom to share, and they held up their glasses in the air. "To the newlyweds," he said, looking at his glass with great tenderness. "May they be as rich as my wine." As an afterthought, he raised his glass to the portraits of Lenin and Gorbachev that hung on the wall, then downed the drink, and everyone applauded while Hanna and Ihor shared their measly glass. Oleh grabbed his bottle before anyone else could demand a shot and was hardly seen the rest of the night.

Nobody complained about the quantity or quality of the food: pork *kovbasa,* chicken, *kapusta, pyrohy,* borsch, caviar from the Black Sea, and several tortes made in the famous "Kyiv style," with thin, crisp wafers layered between rich icings of coffee, chocolate and lemon butter. The sweets were arranged next to a huge silver-plated samovar that once belonged to Evdokia's great-aunt, a serf who had probably stolen it from her master. And Marusia's beautiful wedding bread was given an honored place in the center of the wedding party table where everyone could see it. She tried not to notice who was eating the bread and how often, but her eyes too frequently drifted to the table.

The small wedding band played a waltz, and Marusia was surprised to see Yurko dancing with Hanna again, for the third time.

"Well, he suddenly likes to dance," Zosia said.

"Here, darling. Have some torte. This one has walnuts in it. . . ."

"He complains that he's too tired to go to this and now he's the belle of the ball." Zosia sat down, crossed her legs and nervously jiggled her foot.

"Look, they're finished. Here he comes."

Yurko wiped his head with a blue cotton handkerchief. His face was flushed from the exertion of the dance and the clamminess of the hall. He smiled brightly at Zosia.

"Having a good time?" Zosia said.

"Not bad. Where are the children?"

"Oh, so now you're worried about them? I'm surprised you remembered you're a married man with children."

"They're fine, Yurko," Marusia cut in. "They're with the other children. See—at that table, eating cake."

The familiar opening notes of the *kryvyi tanet* began. "Let's dance this one," Zosia commanded.

Yurko took off his suit jacket, half-hung it on a chair and sat down. "I'm a little tired," he said. He loosened his tie. "It's too fast for me."

Zosia jumped up. "Oh, so because I want to dance, you're tired. But with that whore, you're ready to join the Bolshoi Ballet."

"Look, I already danced with you. . . ."

"And with every pretty girl under thirty."

He stood up. He helped himself to a glass full of carbonated sugar water and downed it. "Remember, Zosen'ka—you wanted me to come to this stupid thing. So I'm here. I don't care if you ask someone else to dance. Go ahead."

"I want to dance with *you!*"

"Let's go," he said wearily. Marusia watched as he and Zosia held hands and rather stiffly whirled out on the dance floor until it was time to switch partners. She turned away when she saw her son paired up with Hanna yet again. Zosia stamped her foot and abruptly left her new dancing partner, one of Ihor's ushers who was too

35

drunk to notice her departure, delighted to twirl around by himself.

After the dance, Yurko found his wife alone, sulking on a bench against a wall, her head bent down. "I didn't plan it," he pleaded. He unbuttoned the top of his shirt and loosened his tie. He sniffed himself and noticed that his shirt was soaked. "I smell worse than a cow in heat. Hardly sexy . . ." He chuckled.

"You're so awful to me." She started to cry without looking at him.

"Oh, come on. You're acting worse than the children. I swear, you're such a baby."

She stood up and grabbed a half-eaten plate of torte that someone had earlier abandoned. "If that's how you see me . . . then here." Zosia dumped the plate on his head and trotted away from him. The sticky icing hung on his damp shirt like brightly colored confetti.

"Well, I guess you're finished with dessert," said Father Andrei, who had been leaning against the wall, and witnessing the scene. He handed Yurko a flimsy paper napkin shaped like a triangle.

"My wife is crazy, Father."

The priest laughed. "Well, I'd like to stay for more excitement, but I'm off for the night shift. I'm getting a lift in my cousin's car."

"You're on for the night too? I might as well go with you. I'm through having a good time here, that's for sure."

"Come with us. He's meeting me in a few minutes outside."

Yurko looked for his mother to tell her he was going. Everyone in the packed hall had clustered into a tight circle around the bride, her mother, Evdokia and some of Hanna's girlfriends.

He found Marusia and squeezed his way between the guests to get to her.

"*Mamo,* I'm leaving now for work. I'm getting a ride to the plant with the priest, so I don't have to wait for the bus." He kissed his mother's forehead.

Marusia held on to his arm. "Where's your jacket? Never mind, I'll find it later. See you tomorrow, darling. I'll tell Zosia you left. Don't worry, things will look better. You'll see."

Yurko didn't hear much of what she said because the band had struck up again. Hanna sat on a velvet cushioned chair in the center of the room. Her friends and mother took off her veil, and Evdokia unplaited the new bride's hair. Yurko kissed his mother again and left just as they were putting a paisley fringed babushka on Hanna's head. "You're a married woman now," her grandmother said. "No more fancy things without a fight from now on!" Everyone laughed except Evdokia, who cried out several times, "My baby," and smothered Hanna's face with kisses.

The guests gathered around Hanna and offered her presents of money. Marusia took out one *karbovanets* she kept deep in her sweater pocket. "For luck," she sighed, and smiled at Hanna when it was her turn to throw the money into a pot. Married people need it more than anyone, Marusia thought to herself. She cast a disapproving glance at Hanna's new husband, who was huddled in a corner with a young woman and laughing more than he should have been.

THE BAND PLAYED until almost midnight. Marusia watched as Zosia lifted her tiny son and danced with him. Little Tarasyk, his face smeared with cake crumbs, was half-asleep in his mother's arms. Katia was dancing a fast polka with another little girl, her long blond hair and satin ribbons flying wildly as she galloped the length of the hall with her friend. Finally they collapsed on the floor laughing because the twirling had made them dizzy.

Past midnight, Marusia and her daughter-in-law collected the sleepy children and headed home. Marusia yawned and was proud to know that all of the *korovai* was eaten, that not a crumb was left to take back with her.

Tarasyk murmured and woke up in the crisp air. "He can walk a little bit," Zosia suggested. Marusia held both of the children's hands and started to make up a story. "Once there was a beautiful little girl named Katia, and a handsome young boy named Tarasyk who danced all night at a magic wedding feast given by the queen of the *Lisovi*. The *Lisovi*, as you know, are the spirits of the forest. Well, the queen fell in love with a wolf who was really the lost king of the caves a long time ago. . . ."

ZOSIA LAGGED BEHIND her family. She dragged her husband's sweat-stained jacket on the ground, thinking about why she was never happy with any man in her life. She was attractive, she was fun, at least she was when she didn't have to worry about her job, or the children or Yurko's cold ways. If he weren't such a bore, such a know-it-all, she might try to be faithful to him. Now, her current lover had left her. She had this new baby to think about. How could she convince Yurko that it might be his after all, when they hadn't made love in so long? How would he take the news if he knew the truth? Would he kill her and the other man? He's too much of a coward, she fumed.

The wedding had depressed her, and she vowed to herself that she wouldn't go to the reception tomorrow. Why are these stupid weddings three days long, she wondered. Once they stop celebrating then it gets bad, so I guess they have to get as much fun as they can out of it before things go to hell. . . .

She kicked at a stone and felt the toe of her nylons rip. I'm too old to have a good time anymore, she told herself, noticing that her short, cracked fingernails looked blue in the twilight. I'm old and ugly and stuck, stuck, stuck. She shivered and put Yurko's jacket around her shoulders. Hugging it closer to her bare arms, she caught a whiff of his cologne—an awful Polish import called "Steve." Then she remembered his real, natural body scent that was so familiar to her—a fragrance similar to damp mushrooms in a dark forest—and how her own lush, wet body was anointed by his scent whenever he lay on top of her. And she suddenly felt very sorry for him and wished that she could love him again.

THE CHILDREN DIDN'T fuss or coax their *Baba* to let them stay up longer as they usually did. Marusia pulled the divan out and made up their beds. Their heads hit the soft down pillows, and they slept hard and still. Marusia was exhausted but managed to get through her nighttime prayers. She heard Zosia pacing around in the kitchen, opening cabinet doors, looking for something. But long after Zosia went to bed, Marusia herself was restless and slept badly. After rolling about for what seemed like hours, she decided to get up. Too many sweets, she thought, rubbing her swollen gums against her tongue. That's what I get for breaking the Lenten fast. She shuffled into the kitchen and found the sage and mint spirits she had bought from Slavka Lazorska years ago and dabbed the pungent liquid on her gums. Next, she took a clove from one of her spice bottles, bit into it and let a piece seep into a cracked molar before finally brewing a tea with hops and going back to her bed.

Marusia glanced at her clock. It was after one in the morning. Gradually, her pain eased and she was able to slip into a dream. In it, she was trapped inside a fog of black clouds, with windstorms kicking up all around her. She was looking for the front door to her house, but couldn't find it, and she screamed for someone to help her. She found a window and saw her neighbors' homes uproot and roll away like tumbleweed. Then she saw the Virgin Mary arising out of a white mist, dressed in blue robes and a long black veil, coming toward her with Her arms out, ready to catch something or someone.

Chapter 4

THE NEXT DAY was a Saturday. Marusia awoke
earlier than usual. The sun had just appeared in the
sky, but the hazy gray clouds screened its light. Marusia
slowly lifted herself out from beneath the high folds
of the goose down *peryna,* careful not to wake the children, who were snoring peacefully nearby, their mouths
open and translucent eyelids shut. Marusia stretched and
yawned and wondered if Yurko had returned. She hadn't
heard him come in and thought that maybe she had slept
soundly after all. But her gums still ached. It's only a matter of time, she thought, before the few good teeth she
had left would have to be replaced by more gold ones.

Marusia prayed fervently to the Blessed Virgin that
morning because she suddenly remembered seeing
Mary in her dream. Then she put on her tattered cor-
duroy house slippers. The soft flapping sound of the slip-

pers hammering against her callused heels echoed its way into the kitchen, where she warmed up some water in a pot for her morning cup of instant coffee and chicory. She rinsed her mouth with warm salt water to soothe her swollen gums and this time plugged her aching tooth with salt pork. "Ukrainians and their salt pork." She smiled to herself. "Scratch a Ukrainian, find salt pork."

Zosia peered into the kitchen. "Oh, *Mamo,* it's you," she said. "I thought it might be Yurko." Her eye makeup was smeared and her face looked puffy.

"No. Maybe he's working overtime."

Zosia grabbed the sides of her neck with both hands as though she were about to choke herself and massaged the base of her skull. "I feel sick."

"Of course you do, darling. You're going to be a mother again."

"Don't remind me," Zosia snapped. "That's all I need on top of everything else." She poured some of the boiling water into a cup and dropped in a small handful of dried spearmint leaves.

"I'll wake the children up," Marusia said, afraid to upset her daughter-in-law. "I'll take them to school. Good thing it's a school day. This way you can rest. Then we can all go to the second wedding reception at Hanna's today."

"I don't care to go anywhere. I'll stay home and wait for Yurko."

THE DAY PASSED quietly. Tarasyk stayed home because he didn't get enough sleep and Katia came home early from school because her teacher was ill and dismissed the class. She and Tarasyk played outside in their garden and Katia saw three helicopters in the sky. "You know what those are?" she asked the little boy. "Robots that fly like birds, and they're looking for children to take away. . . ." Tarasyk ran into the house and hid in the pantry for hours before anyone noticed he was missing.

That afternoon, Marusia was the only one from her family who attended the second reception at the *klub*. The children were too tired and Zosia was too angry. Just as well, thought Marusia, who was soon bored watching the young people dance to their awful, loud pop music.

On her way back home that evening, Marusia noticed how odd the sky looked—it was lit up in the distance the way she remembered the wartime sky, when the Germans bombed the villages. Or maybe it was what Zosia called the northern lights, the flashes of color that appeared in a freak sky. Or maybe an electrical storm in the woods somewhere. She rushed home to ask Zosia or Yurko about it, but everyone was asleep except for Bosyi, who whimpered near the door to let Marusia know that her son had not yet returned home.

THE NEXT DAY was Palm Sunday. Though the church bells did not ring as they usually did for the eight o'clock Mass, the only service of the day, several old people were in attendance. No one expected Hanna and her new husband to appear, because no one expected any of the younger people to show up on holy days, especially when they fell on Sundays. And since Marusia knew that the teachers would ask which students had attended church, it was a good idea not to include her grandchildren in the service because they would only get into trouble, and then Zosia would growl at her for being "so stubbornly primitive."

Marusia stood near the back of the church with Slavka Lazorska and the others. They waited with armfuls of pussy willows, as was the custom. Palms were impossible to get. Father Andrei did not appear to open the altar doors of the iconostasis. He was late, which wasn't surprising since he was probably working overtime at the plant. But when it got to be almost nine o'clock, the women began to whisper among themselves. Paraskevia was especially upset. Father Andrei, her son, had not returned home after his shift ended on Saturday morning. He would not miss a Sunday service unless he was arrested or ill, and yesterday he had missed performing two afternoon wedding ceremonies. She moved to the back of the church, apart from the rest, where she knelt very low on the ground, bowed her head and prayed deeply, her eyes closed.

"I don't think he's coming," said Evdokia. She looked at the watch pinned to her cable-knit sweater.

"We should start by ourselves," said Maia Medvid'. She nudged her husband, Stepan, who hesitantly walked up to the altar, pinched his thumb and the first two fingers together of his right hand, and crossed himself in the Eastern Orthodox manner. He opened the golden doors of the iconostasis. Another elder lit the thin orange candles that stood in front of the icons.

"Hey, Yulia, maybe you should sing," Evdokia said to the tall woman leaning against one of the wooden beams in the center of the church. Long ago, during Stalin's regime, Yulia Pan'kovych had been about to begin training as a mezzo-soprano with the Kyiv Opera when she was arrested and exiled to Siberia for refusing to denounce her music professor, who was accused of teaching anti-Soviet songs. Yulia was well into her seventies, but despite her humped back, her voice was still mellow and resonant, and it reverberated as she sang the somber Lenten hymns. The others in the small gathering of old women and their husbands joined in, except for Paraskevia, who was still on her knees swaying and mumbling the prayer of repentance and beating her slightly sunken chest with her yellow fist.

When they finished the songs, the worshippers lingered together a little longer, praying silently for hope and courage, for loved ones, living and dead, and for the Union—such as it was. Some of them stood and prayed, as there were no benches. Others knelt, kissing the floor. They rose and, at the holy water font near the door, blessed the pussy willows. Then the candles were extinguished and the altar doors closed. It was time for everyone to leave and the church to be locked.

Paraskevia was the last to go. Marusia waited for the old woman to finish her prayers before tapping her shoulder. Tears flooded the older woman's little peanut eyes, and Marusia helped her stand up on her feet.

"God grant you peace," Marusia said.

Paraskevia shook her head and wiped her eyes with her sleeve. They blessed themselves with holy water and walked arm in arm outside into the humid day.

Paraskevia couldn't help crying. "The end of the world. Taste the air. It's not the same. And my son is gone."

Marusia flicked her tongue out for a second. The air did taste different, like steel. She watched Evdokia do the same.

"*Feh!*" Evdokia grimaced, then rushed to Lazorska. "Hey, *Pani Dokhtor,* my eyes are itchy and watering." She saw that Lazorksa's eyes were just as red.

"Something in the air. Maybe pollen. It's spring, after all," the healer said.

"And my old man also gets such horrible hay fever. . . . What cure do you have for it?"

Before Lazorska could answer, Paraskevia released herself from Marusia's arm and yelled out to the group, "*Trahedia!* Tragedy! Go home and hug your grandchildren! Save yourselves from this crooked generation because it's the end of the world!" She turned away and kept shouting and beating her chest with her fist while scuttling down the path leading back to her lonely house.

"She's getting crazier than ever," said Evdokia.

From her oilcloth shopping bag, Slavka Lazorska fished out a dried sunflower head that was still rich with black seeds. She pulled some out of their husks and passed them to the other women. "Paraskevia is a wise woman. She knows things I never heard of." She spat the seed shells out. "But admit it, here we are in God's own backyard, and we are all suffering from some devil's curse in the air."

"Maybe she's just worried about her son," Maia put in, and Marusia wondered if Yurko was all right. He would surely be home by now.

"I suppose the priest was too tired to come today," another woman said.

"Well, when he came to Hanna's reception, he danced his curly head off," Evdokia said. "Everyone saw. . . ." She was looking around for her own husband, who was smoking a forbidden cigarette with some of the men but stopped when he saw her frowning at him. He angrily took out his empty pipe and sucked on it.

Evdokia ran after him with a pussy willow. "I'm not hitting you, the pussy willow is—Easter will be here a week from today!"

"Ow, she's beating me! Ow!" Oleh shuffled away from his wife and smiled. "Help me!"

Everyone laughed at the childish custom which no one fully understood, but enjoyed nonetheless. Some of the men gently tapped their wives with the pussy willows. Marusia tapped Evdokia, who giggled.

After a while, Yulia Pan'kovych cut in. "Did anyone hear a terrible noise Saturday night? It woke me up! I swear my bed was shaking."

Some of the women nodded their heads. "It might have been shooting," Maia timidly offered. The women laughed. "No, really. I remember during the war when a man shot his ex-wife and her new husband on their wedding night. It was terrible."

"Well, unfortunately my granddaughter's new husband is still walking the earth," Evdokia said. "Unless Hanna shot him. And who would blame her."

The women chatted about the weddings they'd attended the day before and what times the Sunday receptions were to occur, but they disbanded early because they were uneasy and wanted to be at home.

On the way, Marusia worried over Paraskevia's bitter words. She was disturbed that even Lazorska was aware of some unknown evil intruding on them. Her eyes smarted and teared, and the metallic taste in her mouth grew stronger. "Feh," Marusia spat, "it's this pollution. Too many of those damn factories around here." She wiped her eyes and felt relieved to be at her gate.

She saw that Katia was playing tag with some other children near her neighbor's front garden. Tarasyk was playing quietly by himself with a small shovel and a mound of dirt in the garden. They didn't seem to be bothered by the air.

Zosia was in the kitchen busily washing Yurko's suit jacket with the thick bar of yellow laundry soap. Her cigarette dangled from her mouth, and the ashes were scattered over her housecoat. She seemed crazed and kept striking the lump of heavy wet wool against the hard sink over and over as though she were beating a demon out of a possessed soul.

Chapter 5

YURKO DID NOT come home until late Monday afternoon. He acted as though his mind was caught in a daze. He ignored everyone's anguish over his absence while he slowly and mechanically peeled off his blue overalls and work boots. He drank three glasses of tepid water and shuffled to his room, where he tumbled into bed and then cried out for more water. Marusia brought him a pitcher's worth, which he drank until his throat convulsed. He coughed some of the liquid up over the covers. "*Mamo,* my throat is so dry. My eyes are burning."

"You need sleep," Marusia said. She felt his hot head with her hand. "I'll get a cool towel."

"At least one of us can sleep. . . ." Zosia grumbled. She was in their room, changing into her blue work fatigues.

"Zosia, listen to me," Yurko said in a hoarse voice. "Don't go. There's been an accident at the plant."

"What accident?" Zosia snapped. "Nobody's said anything."

"Listen to me. Something worse than a fire happened. Nobody knows . . . it's the worst I've ever seen. Something . . ."

Zosia moved over to the bed and bent down near her husband. She realized how bleary-eyed he looked. His face was ashen except for his cheeks and nostrils, which were ruddy in the way they used to get whenever he was out too long in the sun. "What do you mean?" she said more gently.

"I don't know. But there were fires. . . ." Yurko coughed and fell back on the pillows, closing his eyes.

"Easy, *sonechko*," Marusia said, stroking his hair. "I myself heard about a fire when I waited in line at the co-op this morning. And Father Andrei never returned home after the wedding reception. We missed him at Mass yesterday. Maybe you've seen him, Yurko?"

"Don't bother Yurko about that kind of thing, *Mamo*," Zosia said, retreating to her dresser and the large gilt-framed mirror hung over it. The dresser was a clunky piece of furniture that Yurko had taken from his mother's room when he first married Zosia and brought her to this house. Zosia had arranged her few precious cosmetics on a blue and yellow embroidered flaxen towel she had made as a child growing up in Siberia.

Zosia frowned at the plastic tortoiseshell case that held the last few portions of crumbling face powder.

"So, it's nothing special when someone comes home late from a shift, especially if something unusual happens." She powdered her face, then dabbed her cheeks with a sheet of blotting paper she had stolen from work. "Look, Yurko disappeared for two whole days, but he's here. The priest is probably back now, too."

"There were fires," Yurko insisted. Marusia helped him pull himself higher against the pillows behind his back. "Smoke all over. Like a war. I went to Prypiat', to inspect an electrical station. But we all heard the explosion. The ground shook. The sky lit up. Horrible . . ."

"Don't worry, dear," Marusia said. "I'm getting a towel for your head. Cool down, then talk." She tried to catch her daughter-in-law's eye before she left the bedroom, but Zosia was absorbed in dusting her eyelids with a sable artist's brush dipped in light blue eye shadow with bits of silver sparkles in it—"like mica," one of the engineers at the plant had joked when he first saw it shine on her eyes.

"When did this happen?" Zosia asked after they were alone. She moved over to sit on the edge of their bed and raked her stiff, snarly hair with a brush. Her hair snapped with electricity as she tilted her head down on her chin and forced the underside of her hair up and over her face.

"Saturday morning. After I left you at the reception. About two o'clock. I had to go and help put the fires out. Got as far as the gates, but the stink got to my chest. Knocked me out. They took me to Prypiat'. That's where I was all this time." He coughed again. "The medic said I was fine. To get some rest. So, I'm home."

"It's still on fire?" she asked. She was concentrating on pulling off the loose strands of hair caught from the bristles of her brush and dropping them on the floor.

He groped for her hand and pulled her closer to him. "Don't go. Not now. Let them put it out for good."

Zosia pulled away from him and stood up. "But nobody has said anything official about it. Anyway, there's always a backup system. Something goes wrong, there's an alarm and other units kick in."

Marusia returned with a large pink terry washcloth and gently pressed it against Yurko's forehead.

"Did you hear anyone say anything official about an explosion, *Mamuniu?* Maybe on the radio?"

The old woman shook her head.

"So, things aren't that bad. We're safe. They have to have special backup units at a nuclear power plant." Marusia was devoting all her attention to her son. "*Mamo,* did you hear what I said? There's always a backup system."

"Fine then, but people still get hurt on the job," Marusia said. "Workers get sick lifting heavy equipment, especially the women, who shouldn't be doing such things." She glared at Zosia.

"Yurko is not a child, and he's stronger than a woman. He'll be all right."

"I'm tired," Yurko moaned, and closed his eyes.

"Well, let him sleep," Marusia whispered, and covered Yurko with a blanket. "I'll go and make some soup. But I need more dill. I have to ask our neighbor for some. I'll be back." Marusia was about to say something else, but Zosia pressed a finger to her lips and nodded toward Yurko.

Zosia waited until the old woman left them. She heard the front door close. "Now we'll find out what's really going on," Zosia joked. "She and her nosy girl-friends will get all the news before we hear it on the television."

Yurko threw off the blanket. "Just don't go," he said.

"Of course I wouldn't go—not if there was a real problem. But they would let us know, so there is absolutely nothing to worry about," Zosia said firmly. She was applying the rest of her makeup and tried not to look at Yurko. She had never thought about it much before, but Zosia knew about the common small fires and short circuits and power blackouts that regularly occurred at the Chornobyl plant. She might have easily set something off herself with her cigarettes; everyone always smoked on the job, or drank, or stumbled around half-dead from lack of sleep because sometimes the shifts dragged on for twenty-four-hour stretches. There were too many incompetents in dangerous positions. A fire did not surprise her.

But why did the air taste so bad? She had noticed the difference as soon as she sat outside the previous morning, waiting for Yurko to return home. Why did it have that awful metallic tinge? Maybe because the weather was so uncommonly warm for this time of year. Rotting bundles of hay and cow manure could cause a stench.

Then she thought about the children. They went off to school this Monday morning as usual. Why weren't they sent home if something serious was going on? Everything was always done in the best interest of the children—official Soviet policy. So, if they were allowed to be in school and play in the parks, then things couldn't be that serious.

"I'll be late to work if I don't hurry," Zosia announced to Yurko. "With this new job, I still have a lot to learn." Zosia had been recently transferred to the construction unit and no longer worked with Yurko at the electrical stations. She was now a cement mixer, part of the team building a new nuclear reactor addition. Her salary was almost as large as her husband's, as her job was so physically demanding.

At first Zosia enjoyed mastering the new tedium of running the cement mixers, a skill her latest lover had taught her. She enjoyed the closed-door sessions in this man's office and the impressive supply of American cigarettes and Scotch he shared with her. His attention changed to coldness when Zosia told him about her pregnancy. Of course he denied being distant whenever Zosia confronted him and accused him of not liking her anymore. He was quick enough to kiss her sobbing mouth and dismiss her with a new unopened carton of Marlboros. . . .

Not good enough, Zosia thought to herself. She

fiercely whittled the point of her old dark brown eyebrow pencil with a sharp kitchen knife. Just like him to ignore me now, the bastard. She outlined the fine brown hairs of her eyebrows into severe arches. Yurko's pitiful face stared at her in the mirror, and she wished it were another man's reflection.

"Yurchyk," she said tenderly, turning to him, "I'll be back as soon as I can. Your mother will take care of you." She came near enough to kiss the damp towel that lay askew on his forehead. He shut his eyes and said nothing. She listened to his shallow breathing for a minute before she left him.

Zosia hurried into the kitchen, where she tugged on her boots. She looked into the refrigerator and almost grabbed her lunch of cucumbers and the fresh farmer cheese that Marusia had earlier made. No, she thought, and slammed the refrigerator door. "I'll catch him right before the break and make him take me to eat in the chiefs' dining room. If he's going to leave me, then I should at least get a good dinner out of it. And he's going to pay for a lot more."

She thought hard about how she would meet him face-to-face, what his expression would be and what she was going to say. She thought about these things during the short walk down the dirt path that led to the village center. Her thoughts were interrupted by the stronger taste of the metallic air that bit her tongue and lips. Further down the path and all along the road, Zosia encountered clumps of sticky white foam that had settled on the grass and bushes.

She tried to wipe some of it off her boots against the curb near the bus stand where she and several workers going to Chornobyl waited for the shuttle.

She had to step aside from the cow herd that was on its way to the dairy at the collective farm. Twice a day, the cows walked past Zosia's home.

"*Dobryi den*," a woman with a stick called out to Zosia. "Stinks, doesn't it. Even the cows noticed. Not much milk today." Before Zosia could reply, the woman poked a couple of the cows away from the foam. "Hey, don't eat that! That's from somebody's laundry."

Zosia waited until the herd passed her by. A few of the animals nudged her in greeting, and she patted their rumps and muttered compliments to them as they passed.

The bus did not come. Zosia stood with a group she knew casually. Like Zosia, they were also dressed in blue fatigues and rubber boots, and they all smoked the heavy Soviet cigarettes that burned up too quickly to truly satisfy anyone's craving.

"The bus is never late," said Lesia Narzokina, a woman Zosia admired for her orange lipstick and stylish short red hair.

"It didn't come last night either," said a young man with a blond crew cut and a day's stubble on his chin.

The workers moved away from the curb as two men hosing down the street passed the bus stop. "Why are they doing that?" Zosia demanded.

"They do it on hot days, because the sidewalks get so heated," said the crew cut man, as though he had some authority and knew about such official things.

"But it's not summer," said Zosia. "My husband told me there was a fire at the plant."

"It must have been really something because I heard an explosion like a sonic boom a few nights ago," Lesia added.

"Graphite fires," said the crew cut. "That happens at a nuclear plant. Standard procedure. Nothing to worry about."

"But why doesn't the bus come?" asked Zosia.

Nobody answered. They were too distracted by the sight of Paraskevia Volodymyrivna, who had a large green and orange babushka wrapped around her tiny monkey face, her thin legs encased in heavy woolen stockings and boots, and her body lost in a long black fake lamb's fur coat. The outfit was especially out of place in the warm weather. "You won't have enough water to wash away this sin!" she screamed at the men hosing the streets. The men turned off their hoses for a minute and laughed, then turned their backs toward her and restarted the hoses. Paraskevia was about to strike one of the men but slipped and fell against a gutter, knocking her head on the concrete.

"Look out!" Zosia yelled. She threw her cigarette down and hurried to where the old lady had fallen. Puddles of foam eddied around Paraskevia's small frame.

Zosia ran up to the men with the hoses. She waved her arms in front of them to stop. When they shut off their hoses, Zosia returned to Paraskevia, knelt down and gently lifted the wizened head and loosened her dripping babushka. Her short gray hair felt like the gossamer wool Zosia used to bundle when she was a young schoolgirl working at a collective farm on her summer vacations.

She felt a bump, but no blood, and the old woman's skull between her thin hairs was as tender as a newborn's.

"I'm all right," the older woman said. "Save yourselves." Zosia helped her to stand up and steadied her by holding her bony elbows. "I'm going back to my house," Paraskevia announced. She tied her wet babushka back under her chin.

Zosia gently maneuvered Paraskevia toward the sidewalk and was glad when she didn't cause a fuss. "If you don't mind, I'll walk with you a little bit," Zosia said. "Let me carry your coat." The old lady obliged and allowed Zosia to help her slip out of the sodden, shabby coat. Zosia was surprised at its heaviness.

Paraskevia studied Zosia's face intently with her deep black eyes. "Bless you. You're a good girl after all," she declared.

They walked in silence all the way to the old woman's house. "Will you be all right?" Zosia blurted out once they had reached her gate. "Can I help you bring this coat in? Or is there anything else I can do to help? If you want me to, I mean . . ."

Paraskevia laughed and allowed Zosia to place the dripping coat over her outstretched arms. "I've been taking care of myself for a hundred years. But it's your generation that should get down on your hands and knees and pray that we all come out of this alive."

"Excuse me?"

"Smell the air!"

"Oh, yes. That's the fire. My husband was there and told me about a fire at the plant."

"Why does the air smell like this? You tell me."

"They're putting out the fire."

Paraskevia shook her head. "Fire from hell."

A car horn beeped and a blue car pulled up to them. It belonged to one of Zosia's neighbors who also worked at the plant. A stout man with a mustache rolled down the window from the passenger side of the front seat, and Zosia recognized Maksym, the man who had carried Hanna over the muddy road on her wedding day. "Come on, we've got a ride," he shouted over the loud muffler. "We can still make our shift."

Zosia turned to the old woman. "Are you going to be all right?"

Paraskevia wiped her eyes. "You should ask yourself that question." She made the sign of the cross over Zosia. "God grant you peace and protect you." She freed her small right hand from the coat, firmly grabbed one of Zosia's wrists to make her lean toward her and kissed her. "My life is over." Paraskevia then quickly made the sign of the cross again, spat three times on the ground and went through her front gate where two skinny goats greeted her and followed her into her house.

"Better come now if you're coming," Maksym shouted. Zosia pushed her way into the backseat of the car with two other workers. "You can sit on my lap," joked a man Zosia didn't know.

"Never mind, just move over," she said. She still felt the soft pressure of the old woman's lips on her forehead.

They passed the bus stop and more of the plant workers waiting for the shuttle bus, and the car splashed down the main street where the men with hoses continued to drench the road.

The ride to the plant was only fourteen kilometers but took more than the usual twenty minutes because the main highway leading to Chornobyl was shrouded in smoke. More cars were returning from the plant than going toward it.

"Turn on your headlights," Maksym said to the driver, Borys, who gripped the wheel with his small, pudgy hands. Zosia felt nauseated but rolled her window shut and tried not to breathe. The man next to her started to cough on her face, and she shrank away from him as much as she could by pressing her head against the grimy window.

When they arrived at the plant's gate, they saw dense black smoke and red flames dancing high over the tall watchtowers. Crowds of people in jumpsuits and helmets with eye shields and face masks were chaotically running. A siren sang out, and fire trucks raced toward one of the reactors not far from the building where Zosia worked. Overhead, helicopters flew low over the buildings but didn't land anywhere; they simply hovered in the black air like hornets around a nest.

A man in a helmet pounded on the windshield of their car. Maksym rolled down his window a crack. "Go back, go back, unless you want to help," he shouted through his thin paper mask.

"What can we do?" Maksym asked.

"We need men to collect sand to douse the fires," said the man. "Hurry up, or leave." Then he ran to where another car pulled up.

"I've got to go," Maksym said. "Tell my wife what happened." Zosia and the others in the car watched his huge muscular body pile out of the car, run out and disappear into the dense smoke.

"I'm going too," the man next to Zosia said.

"Me too," said another voice, a large woman Zosia had hardly noticed. "I can't get out on my side. The door's stuck," she yelled, trying to push it open. "You, let us out," she barked at Zosia.

Zosia had to leave the car to let them out, and she coughed violently during the few seconds that she stood in the din.

The woman slammed the door so violently Zosia was unable to open it. In a panic, she tried the passenger side, forced it open and collapsed onto the front seat next to the driver, Borys.

"Listen," Borys said, worried. "You want to go to a hospital or something?"

She shook her head no.

"Well, I'm going back home." He reversed the car and rammed the gate, throwing Zosia's forehead against the dashboard. Her eyes and throat burned, but she felt better with her forehead resting against the soft black vinyl of the glove compartment.

"Hold on," the driver said. Zosia coughed little then, but her breath wheezed and she felt her chest bellow in and out as though a stone on fire were lodged behind her throat.

At last the car pulled up in front of her home. The driver nudged her with his elbow. "Can you make it in by yourself?" he asked. She looked up and saw fear etched in the red crisscrossed lines of his huge round eyes.

She nodded, got out of the car, and then managed to stagger to the front door. She was winded, and her throat was scratchy, but she found she could breathe a little easier. The coughing aggravated her nausea, and she waited a few more seconds until the car screeched away before vomiting into a patch of wild raspberries.

Inside, she realized the metallic smell and a hint of smoke had leaked inside the house. Her knees shook, and she nearly collapsed while shutting the two open windows in the front room.

It was quiet. *"Mamo?"* she called out feebly, starting another coughing fit. There was no answer, only the placid, familiar rhythm of the pink clock ticking on top of the television. It was too early for the children to be home from school. She stumbled to her bedroom, where Yurko still slept and Bosyi still lay on the little lambskin rug by the bed. Zosia was light-headed and shaky from exhaustion, but she managed to pull off her sweaty boots and uniform. She stopped to listen to Yurko's short, rasping breaths coming from deep within his chest be-fore propping one uncertain knee on the bed.

"Stay," she said to the dog, who started to whimper and lick her foot. "You can stay." She briefly touched its head and gently eased herself into the bed next to her husband. She covered both of them with his thin flannel blanket and lifted his head near her shoulder. Her spine tingled a bit each time she felt his shallow breath puff gently on her neck.

Chapter 6

Zosia was flying sky high, deep into the black clouds. Her lightweight body was hurled over a granite wall, but she landed upright on her feet, like a cat. The *chort* stood tall, towering over her. He wore a black robe with a hood like the medieval Western monks she once saw on a television program. The *chort* asked her in a baritone's voice, "If you are to be saved, then what good is the world?"

And Zosia was six years old again. Her hair was in ringlets, and she wore a big white bow pinned to her head exactly like the one her own daughter wore now. She started to cry and pointed to the wall behind her, at the inscriptions from the beatitudes etched in the stone, written in an alphabet she had never seen before, although she was able to read each sentence out loud:

"Blessed are the poor in spirit for theirs is the kingdom of heaven.

"Blessed are the meek, for they shall inherit the earth.

"Blessed are those who hunger and thirst for righteousness, for they shall be satisfied. . . ."

The demon disappeared into a black smoke, and Zosia heard the church bells; not the shallow clanging ones from the village church in Starylis, but the big, resonant bells she remembered from the golden domed church she attended when she was the child of political exiles in Siberia; from the time when she memorized her catechism as though it were her life's calling.

Zosia awoke and remembered her dream. Her arms were still wrapped around her sleeping husband, and they were both wet with sweat. She strained her ears. She heard bells after all, but the sound came from the cowbells Marusia had hung outside their front door because they didn't have a real doorbell.

She put on a robe and stumbled her way to the front door. A little girl in blond braids wearing the bright red scarf and crisp white blouse of the Communist Young Pioneers greeted her. "*Dobryi den'*. Here, take this." She held up a waxed paper envelope.

"What is it?" Zosia asked.

"Iodine pills. Because of a fire at the Chornobyl plant. Give one to each member of your family once a day." The little girl turned to go.

"Wait a minute," Zosia said.

"I have to go now," the little girl said impatiently. "Take the pills and you'll feel better."

Zosia watched her skip down the road. She felt weak and sat down outside on the blue-gray slate of the front steps. Her red eyes were heavy with sleep and grit, and she lay her head on her knees, too dizzy to make a move.

MARUSIA FOUND HER keeled over on the steps. "Zosen'ka, wake up!"

Zosia sat upright. Her head ached, and the hand tightly clutching the envelope the girl had given her was numb. "I'm fine."

She saw that Katia was staring at her. Tarasyk began to cry. "Come here, darlings." She brought the children to her chest and hugged them hard, but only the little boy held on to her. Katia wriggled out of her mother's grasp and ran into the house. "Go with your sister," Zosia whispered and dully watched the little boy turn away from her.

"*Bida!*" Marusia cried. "Calamity! We're not supposed to go out of the house today. We have to shut all the windows. I saw the *militsiia* with guns in the village. I was in town getting the children and a *militsioner* yelled into that big megaphone they carry and said we all have to stay in our homes today." Then she remembered, "You're not working? Are you all right?"

Zosia stood up too quickly and had to hold on to Marusia's arm. "I'm a little groggy," she said. "I've had a nap. Yurko is still asleep."

"Thank God for that. He was so tired, poor boy. What do you have in your hand?"

"Oh, I got these a while ago," Zosia said. She handed Marusia the iodine tablets. "Give one to the children and take one yourself. Iodine tablets. For protection. Give one to Yurko if he's awake. Go on, I'll just sit here a few minutes. Then I'll come in."

"Hurry up. The air is so bad. . . ." Marusia looked at Zosia with great concern before briefly touching the top of her head.

Zosia waited until Marusia was out of sight before she allowed herself to succumb to her nausea. I'm going to die, she thought calmly. She was kneeling on the grass, hugging her waist and concentrating on a bee that was hovering in mad semicircles near her head.

She closed her eyes, and her ears were full of the harsh sounds of birds squawking in the linden trees above her. Then she heard Myrrko the cat purr and felt it nuzzle her cheek. "My friend," she said, hugging it close to her. The cat's coarse tongue licked her hand. It pressed its claws into Zosia's sleeves and did not leap out of her arms when she struggled several times to stand before finally regaining her balance. Once in the kitchen, the cat jumped to the floor, paused as though sniffing the air, and quickly darted out. "Looks like kitty isn't hungry. That's new," Marusia said. She was heating a cast-iron pot of barley soup on the woodstove.

A FINE RAIN fell that evening, and Yurko slept hard. Zosia was disturbed in the night by the painful lowing of their cow. Marusia spent the night in the shed, where the cow was expected to birth her calf. "She cries with big round tears in her eyes," Marusia reported to Zosia, who came out to see what the trouble was. "But she doesn't want to give life."

ZOSIA WAS MAKING a cup of instant chicory coffee early the next morning when she heard the cowbells ring again at her front door. This time a man in a blue uniform carrying a shotgun stood in the doorway. He was from the *militsiia*. "*Tovaryshko,* you know about the fire at the plant?"

Zosia pulled the collar of her robe closer to her chin. "Not much." She heard her mother-in-law come into the hallway behind her.

"Nothing to worry about, nothing at all. But for your safety we will be evacuating the residents here. Be ready by five o'clock this afternoon. You'll only be gone for a day or so. Three days at the most."

Marusia peered behind Zosia's shoulder. "Where are we going? I have a cow who is going to give birth any day now. She might have trouble. She did the last time."

"Don't worry, *Babo.* Just keep it away from the grass."

"What does he mean?" Marusia asked Zosia.

"Radiation?" Zosia asked. She wanted someone official to say the word to her face.

"Just a touch. Couldn't be helped. That's normal when there's a fire at the plant. Ask any engineer. It'll pass. Did you get any potassium iodine tablets?"

Zosia perked up at the question. "No," she lied. There were always shortages of such things, and she wanted to get all the medicine she could. Maybe she could sell the tablets in an emergency. Maybe Yurko would need more than his one tablet per day.

The *militsiia* took out the familiar crumpled waxed paper envelope from a pouch strung on his belt. "Here, *tovaryshko*. One a day."

"My husband is ill. We'll probably need more."

"Don't worry. We'll take care of it. Just grab a few things to take with you, stuff you would take for a weekend holiday, then come to the village center and we'll put you on a bus. There are buses going to the hospital, too. You'll be back before you've had time to unpack."

YURKO WAS WEAK and tired, but he moved around the house. He had lost his appetite and ate only a little of the soup Marusia made for him. Zosia was cuddling Tarasyk, who seemed to have an earache. He was crying and fidgety. Katia played silently with her doll in the corner of the kitchen. She refused to change out of her black school uniform with the white lace apron and huge hair bow. Marusia wanted to stay in the shed with the cow, but saw that it was up to her to pack for the family. She managed to fit everyone's overnight clothing into one heavyweight suitcase, the only one she had kept since she was last evacuated during the war.

She had hidden the large, boxy case behind the oak-veneer closet where they stored their clothes. Inside the suitcase, folded with mothballs and a small sachet of lavender, lay some of Marusia's old hand-embroidered blouses made of crepe and linen from when she was a girl. She also kept her wedding costume, now yellowed, and her dead husband's one good dress shirt, which somebody once told her was made of silk. It too was a yellowed white, but it was still as intoxicating to her as when she first saw him in it at their wedding. She held the shirt to her face, and her thoughts drifted to the very painful day he left her for another woman. "After all these years, Antin, I still don't know why. It still grieves my heart. Even in your death, I ask you, why *that* one? Why did you choose that little whore?" She sobbed into the shirt.

"Foolish *baba*," she muttered to herself. "I don't have time to think about foolishness." She found another box to put her old treasures in and slipped it behind the closet. The suitcase was still useful; its handle was firm, and the spring lock worked well enough. She liked the blue satin interior, though it seemed too grand for the threadbare cotton underwear and thin flannel night-clothes she was packing. She didn't know what to pack for Zosia, who was so particular about her things.

Next, Marusia stuffed her canvas shopping bag with heavy glass jars filled with the vegetables she had put up the previous season. For the road, she added two long *kovbasa* sticks, a slab of salt pork, a few tomatoes and cucumbers and a loaf of dark rye bread she had baked earlier in the week. She also pushed in a flask of vodka in case Yurko was still sick and some other little snacks for the children to chew on when they were difficult.

When she was satisfied, she swept the floors, made the beds, and washed the dishes. She put away the stray food, except the scraps she kept out for the dog and cat, who were following her around the house, pacing around her feet until it irritated her. They seemed nervous, and she kept accidentally stepping on their tails.

She went out to the stable to bless her cow. "We'll be back, darling. You'll just have to give birth alone." She hugged its coarse head and cried on the little place between its ears. The cow mooed with pain. It tossed its head and danced around the old woman. "Don't be mad at me. I'm sorry. I don't want to go. But I'll be back in a day or two. Do your best. I'll ask the *militsiia* to take care of you."

Marusia wiped her tears and returned to the house, where she found Yurko sitting in the kitchen, smoking a cigarette and listening to the radio. "Are you feeling better, *sonechko?*" Marusia asked.

His eyes were distant. He seemed distracted by her question. "*Mamo,* it's good that we're leaving." His voice was weak and higher pitched than usual. He turned up the volume of the radio. A static-filled voice was jabbering in Russian about evacuation schedules. Nothing specific was said about the fires or why it was necessary to leave.

Zosia came in. Her face looked paper-white, but

strangely pretty. Marusia pursed her lips when she saw that Zosia wore her amber bracelet and the offensive, whorish high platform shoes she was so proud of, but this was not a time to mention the presents Zosia took from her men friends.

"Come on, darling heart," Zosia called to Tarasyk. The boy ran to his mother and greedily took her hand. He was holding on to a stuffed bunny that had only one eye and half of an ear.

Zosia listened to the broadcast for a minute. "Turn it off. They won't say anything we don't already know. Let's get going."

Marusia was the last to leave the house. She turned off the electric lights and looked around the rooms one more time. At the last minute she almost took her personal icon of the Madonna and Child, but she decided to leave it because it was nailed too tightly into the plaster. For over fifty years, it had hung next to the woodcut portrait of the national poet, Shevchenko. There was no time to pull it off. After all, they'd be back soon enough. "We're waiting, Marusia," Zosia called out from the front yard. Marusia locked the door.

Zosia held each of her children's hands. Marusia started to take the suitcase, but Yurko held it fast by the handle. "I'll take it. You can carry the bag of food," he said. Marusia let him take it from her without protest, but she was worried that he might fall faint on the road to the village. Yurko walked ahead of them, straight and hardly wavering. She wondered if his knees were buckling. He did not greet the neighbors who happened to be walking with them at the same time, leaving Marusia to talk to them and cover up Yurko's rude silence.

She was grateful when they made it into the village center, where several empty buses waited, their doors closed. Everyone who lived in Starylis was standing in unruly lines for their seats. *Militsiia* men and women with shotguns slung on their shoulders stood between the villagers, abruptly answering questions and strutting importantly on the sidewalks.

"*Dobri liudy!* Good people of Starylis," a burly *militsiia* man shouted into a bullhorn. "This evacuation is for your protection. Don't worry, you'll be compensated by our government."

Marusia and her family found themselves in a long line. Yurko put down the suitcase and sat on it. Zosia and the children spread a blanket they had brought with them and sat on it, huddled together. Soon, though, Marusia stood, hoping to seek out some sympathetic official to take care of her beloved cow.

In line, some men were passing a vodka bottle. "Decontaminate yourselves, *tovaryshi,*" they laughed, handing one another a bottle. "Nothing purer. Not even mother's milk."

"This will kill anything! Especially this batch."

"It'll be over in a few days, maybe a week, so drink up now, you'll be back for a fresh bottle," they joked, and the men winked at the younger girls, who flashed quick smiles back at them.

"Well, with so many alcoholics on the job, no wonder there was a fire," a woman was heard to say, which brought out a round of laughter.

"That's right, darling. A bottle of vodka, a hot man, mix them together and poof. . . ." said an old man without front teeth.

"Where are we going, *Babo?*" Katia asked. She was rocking a naked baby doll in her arms. Its blue eyes stared coldly up at the sky.

"We're going for a nice trip to the city." She'd heard on the radio broadcast that they were going to Kyiv, maybe Moscow. Marusia was afraid. She had never been to the big city and dreaded the idea of having to walk the big streets where cars could run you down at a hundred kilometers an hour. How would her son manage that? She glanced at Yurko, who sat with his head bent down. He was ignoring Tarasyk, who tried to sit on his lap. Zosia peered into his face. "You need a doctor." She stood up. "*Mamo,* I'm going to find out if any of these buses go to the hospital." Before Marusia could object, Zosia hurried away from them, and Tarasyk started to cry. "Come here, *soloden'kyi. Tato* is too tired right now. *Mama* will be back soon. Come to *Baba.*" Tarasyk shook his head no, until Marusia coaxed him with some chewy apple slices she had dried the previous winter. "That's my baby," she whispered to the child, who settled down, sucking on the fruit held in his even white baby teeth.

People in line were joking and talking until their attention was drawn to two *militsioner* dragging Paraskevia Volodymyrivna.

"Make way, good people," one of the *militsiia* shouted. As they approached the village center, Paraskevia wrung herself free from her escorts and sat down in the middle of the street.

Two men in front of Marusia guffawed when they saw the scene. "Oh, oh!" one of them said, pointing to a goat who jumped away from a group of *militsiia*.

"Her and her goats! They had a hell of a time getting her out of her cellar with those animals," an old woman declared.

The crowd laughed and watched three more uniformed men try to corral the goat after it butted one of them in the rear. A woman *militsiiantka* threw rocks at it, which steered the animal back on the dirt road toward its home.

"Look, they're hurting the goat," Katia cried out. "Why are they doing that?"

"Now behave yourself, *babo!*" one of the *militsioner* yelled at Paraskevia. He and another man helped her roughly to her feet. She spat in his face.

Marusia darted her way through the crowds close enough to yell out to the old woman. "Paraskevia," she said. "Please wait with me and my family. They won't hurt you."

Paraskevia did not recognize her friend and shouted wildly, "I'd rather die here. This is my home. My home, you bandits! I have to wait for my son to come back." The old woman started to cry. "He is the priest. No one else is here for him to come home to. Just me."

Marusia heard someone honking a horn. A driver was in one of the buses, waiting for his instructions.

"All right, get her in first," a *militsioner* shouted. Two men forcibly lifted the old woman and carried her into the bus.

"No! No! I want to go home," she protested.

Marusia turned away when she saw Paraskevia's tattered slip hanging out in full view as they hoisted her into the bus.

"Hey, don't be so rough on the *babtsia*," shouted a blond-haired man in a torn T-shirt. His arms were stained with tattoos.

"You don't know what a mean old lady she is," the *militsioner* with the bullhorn answered. He wiped his perspiring face with his wide black tie. "It took four of us to get her out of her cellar, and she had six goats with her."

"What a hero!" the tattooed man shouted. "Is that who we have protecting us? Even the old ladies are tougher than our dear little policemen." Everybody laughed.

"All right, your attention now," the *militsioner* brusquely shouted into his bullhorn. "Keep the lines moving. There is room for everyone on these buses." As he spoke, more drivers in black leather caps strolled leisurely to their buses, sat down in their seats, and waited for their passengers.

Zosia returned and led her family to another area of the town square where they stood with other groups of villagers. Suddenly, the pace of the lines picked up and moved faster than Marusia was used to, and she panicked when it was her turn.

"Wait a minute." Marusia turned from the bus doors.

"*Mamo,* come on," Zosia said, helping her children to climb in while Yurko struggled with the large suitcase.

"I'll be right there." She forfeited her place in line and went up to the officer with the bullhorn. "Excuse me, please . . . I have a cow. . . ."

"Don't worry about your stupid animals. I'm so sick of these damn old ladies and their animals. . . ."

"But my cow was supposed to calve. She might have a problem. . . ."

"You'll be compensated. We have to save people first." He dismissed her with a shove toward the bus. Marusia's heart sank, and she had half a notion to sneak back to her house and wait for her family to return in a few days. But then she thought of how they forced Paraskevia.

Marusia searched for her bus. They all looked the same until she saw Zosia standing on the steps and blocking others from entering.

"*Woo-uh,*" Marusia shouted, shoving her way back into the right line. "*Wooh!* Wait for me!" Zosia was arguing with a man who tried to pull her off the steps. "I'm here," Marusia said, relieved.

"Come on, *Mamo!*" She pushed the surly man to the side and helped the old woman on. "Good thing you came. Otherwise I'd have to kick him where it hurts, the bastard."

"I'd like to see you try, you whore," he said.

"Why bother, there's nothing there to kick," Zosia retorted.

"Oh yeah! I'll show you what I got!" He started to unzip his pants.

"Hey you, not here," cried a *militsioner*. "You can't piss in the middle of a street. Against the law!"

"Arrest me then! To the Gulag! *Davai!* Come on."

"Drunk, too," he called to another *militsioner*. They argued and shouted at one another while the others in line shoved in.

The bus was packed with more than three times as many passengers as seats. Old people crouched in the aisles. Marusia and Zosia sat on top of their bundles with the children on their laps near the front of the bus. Yurko stood over them, holding on to one of the hanging straps, his eyes closed, struggling just to stay upright.

The minute his own space was invaded by bobbing heads and elbows jamming into his back, the driver slammed the doors. He didn't care that he might have cut off a part of a family, perhaps separating a parent from a child. Once he saw that his own legs might be cramped by too many bundles, he was ready to roll. Doors shut, he zoomed the bus out of town.

Yurko appeared as lifeless as a corpse on a gallows as he swayed with each jerking motion of the vehicle.

"Sit down, *bratiku*," said a tired voice. A bald man with an eyepatch tapped Yurko on the shoulder. "You, please sit down." He stood up and gave Yurko his seat.

"Thank you," Yurko said, embarrassed. He felt that he should offer his seat to Zosia or his mother, but he felt weak and truly wanted to sit down. "I've been ill," he confided, ashamed of himself.

"Really?" said the bald man, waiting for more. He tried to open the window behind Yurko, but all the windows were stuck shut.

"From the plant. It's bad. . . ." Yurko suddenly turned his head toward the window. Outside, a pack of dogs was following the bus. The dogs howled after their masters.

"Look at that, they want to leave, too," said the bald man.

"It's Bosyi, my dog," Yurko mumbled. He wasn't exactly sure if Bosyi was in the pack, but he liked to think he saw him one last time. He had hardly patted his head before he left, although Bosyi whined and nudged him and licked his face almost as if he was desperate. "Good-bye, my friend," Yurko said to himself.

"Damn, stupid animals," the bus driver shouted, stepping on the gas. He was an ugly man in his twenties with a bad complexion who wore his black leather cap jauntily perched on the side of his head. He lit a cigarette and turned on a portable radio that was hooked up to the dashboard. Russian rock music blared over the hacking coughs and whimpering children.

The dogs followed the bus, yelping and whining, but gave up once the vehicle picked up speed on the smoother, paved highway. Yurko sank back into the torn leather seat.

Marusia looked over to her son but could not see him behind the crowded travelers standing over her. She glanced out the window and caught a passing glimpse of a small group of young men burying their cars and television sets deep in the ground on the town's outskirts.

"We should have done that," a woman behind Marusia said.

"What for? We'll be back in a couple of days," said someone else, probably her husband.

The bus took a back road, shifting into second gear to pull up a steep hill. It almost turned over when the driver swerved into the opposite lane to pass the slower buses in front of him. He beeped his horn and swore out loud.

"Sorry, darling," someone said. Yurko's eyes snapped open. His upper lip was bristling with sweat. He unbuttoned the top few buttons of his shirt, hoping to breathe easier in the stench of the diesel fumes.

The bus slowed down in front of the *kolhosp*. Three tractors were mowing the fields for hay. Mounds of grain were piled by the side of the road, and strong women in bright head kerchiefs were emptying the sacks and handing the depleted bags to a man with a pickup truck.

"What are they doing?" someone wanted to know. "Why are they wasting food like that?"

"They need the sacks for sand. To put out the fire," said the driver to no one in particular. He stopped the bus near one of the women on the roadside. She was younger than the others and wore a pair of faded jeans that stuck tight to her ample thighs and backside.

The bus driver opened the doors. "Hey, beautiful," he shouted in Russian to the girl. "Forget that work and come with me to Kiev. I'll buy you a mink coat."

She laughed and took off her kerchief, stroking back her straw-blond hair. "Thanks, but we're going on another bus after we finish here," she said. Then she giggled and sauntered closer to the bus door, where she posed with one foot on the bottom step.

"Good, then meet me at the relay station tonight in Kiev. I stashed away a bottle of the best *sovietskoye champanskoye* and I got a nice bottle of perfume for you . . . from Paris."

She giggled again. "Get out of here! Paris! Who do you think you're kidding!"

"All right, Prague, then. But you should pour it over your beautiful neck tonight. Or better yet, let me do it." He blew her a kiss and put his cigarette back in his mouth before closing the doors. The girl waved, and the driver's eyes kept staring into the rearview mirror until she was completely out of sight.

Chapter 7

THE BUS THAT carried Marusia and her family
ended up in front of a hospital near the center of Kyiv in
the early hours of the evening. The trip took longer than
usual because the driver made several more stops along
the way to talk and flirt with other women. Finally, when
an angry female passenger in the back of the bus yelled
at him to stop pimping or she would throttle him with
her fists and drive the bus herself, he made no more de-
tours and took them directly to their stop.

Marusia was awed when she saw the city's skyline
for the first time. She watched in respectful silence as
the bus turned down various streets and boulevards.
Kyiv was so imposing with its broad high-rises, so important with its spacious gardens filled with manicured
hedges and colorful rows of tulips and elaborate war
monuments, and the heavily sculpted statue of Lenin
that was so prominent in the center of the main street.

Large red banners bearing slogans of the Revolution in both Russian and Ukrainian billowed high above the immaculate white sidewalks that Marusia had heard were kept in that pristine condition by hundreds of old women and their brooms.

Crowds of weary people were already waiting in long lines outside the emergency ward entrance. They had come from other villages that surrounded Chornobyl and had been dropped off long before Marusia's bus arrived. They were still waiting their turns to be processed by some official and to be given a place where they might sleep that night.

Except for her family, Marusia lost sight of the familiar faces from the bus ride. Nor did she see any of her friends and neighbors; everyone here seemed to be a stranger to her.

The family joined a group of evacuees from another village called Narodochyi because Zosia insisted that the lines in that group were not as long. Actually, Zosia wanted to avoid running into her ex-lover from the plant or other people who knew about them. She would hate to have to explain things to Yurko and Marusia now.

Marusia was made more nervous by the fearful and uncertain voices around her. Instinctively she knew that survival depended upon a different set of rules than anything she had known back in her little village. She allowed Zosia to try to lead the family to safety—at least until things made more sense to her.

Zosia carried Tarasyk. Katia held on to Marusia's hand, and Yurko straggled behind them, half carrying, half pushing the suitcase. They ambled between groups of people crammed together on the sidewalks jealously guarding their few possessions and protecting the little space they had secured in the lines.

Zosia went boldly up to the doors of the emergency room and announced that her entire family was contaminated with radiation. They must be let in immediately.

A toady little man who was in charge of the doors was either intimidated by her temper or by her good looks. He didn't argue with her, but opened the doors and even smiled at Zosia. Inside, more people waited in more lines, many too tired and dejected to stand. Babies were howling, men were coughing, women were shouting. People were sprawled out everywhere on the floor and propped against the walls. Some luckier folks were asleep on stretchers and on abandoned examination tables.

Marusia's sharp eyes found an area on the far side of the packed room, near the entrance leading into a corridor. She and Katia quickly rushed to claim their patch of wall and carpet. She made Katia sit on the floor, then waved for Zosia, Tarasyk and Yurko to join her.

Marusia smiled shyly at the group near her spot, a young couple hushing and rocking their colicky twins. Both of the babies were crying at once. "Nice voices," Marusia said over the babies' howls. "They'll be great singers someday." It was her way of being apologetic to her neighbors, since she had taken away some of their space and privacy, such as it was. She clicked her tongue happily at the infants, who ignored her and cried louder.

The mother nodded. She was dark, like a Georgian, and yet looked Slavic because of her blue eyes and heart-shaped face. Zosia and Tarasyk plopped down near Marusia. Yurko set the suitcase down as though it might break and then sat on it. He looked at the young mother of the twins, whose skin was the same abnormal tan color as his own, and he quickly dropped his eyes away from her.

"My babies are tired," the young woman said. She had a slight lisp.

Yurko ignored her. He didn't want to look at her again. He knew everything about her and her suffering because he felt it deep in his own blood and skin. He wanted to hold his own children close to him for a little bit and hug them near his heart so that he could feel their innocent sweet breath on his polluted face. He sat and watched his son, who was in a bad temper and fought with his mother as she changed his wet pants, and then he turned to look at his daughter, sitting on the plump, safe lap of his own mother, and he felt a wave of remorse for his wasted life.

Yurko's head sank lower on his chest. He blinked back his tears. To steady himself, he lit a cigarette and tried to concentrate on the smoke circling before his smarting eyes.

An obese nurse in a white duster and a paper-thin coned cap stood in the center of the room and clapped her hands. "*Uh-vah-ha! Uh-vah-ha!* Pay attention, *tovaryshi!* Everyone will be taken care of. You will be fed and given a place to sleep tonight. Everybody will be processed according to their number."

"What number?" Marusia anxiously whispered to Zosia. "Did we get a number?"

"Don't worry, we will," Zosia said confidently.

The nurse waddled to a wooden desk at the far end of the room. She gruffly shook the shoulder of a man with a thick growth of beard who had fallen asleep on top of her desk. He awoke in surprise and jumped to his feet when he saw the nurse looming over him. She heaved herself into her seat behind the desk, took out a thick notebook, a pen and a full bottle of ink from a drawer, and spread them all on the desk with great deliberation. The room quieted down. She looked up and bellowed, "Number one . . ."

Katia had to go to the bathroom. Zosia foraged around the room until she found an empty specimen bottle beneath an examination table. "Come on darling," she coaxed, "just squat and do it into the bottle."

"I don't want to," Katia said, and started to cry.

Tarasyk fell asleep with his thumb in his mouth on the floor next to his father, who ventured a slight caress over the boy's golden hair. Zosia gently took the blanket that covered him. "Here, a little modesty," she said, holding up the blanket. "You go behind it and pee into the bottle. No one will see you."

"I'll help you, dear," Marusia offered.

"No, I'll do it," Katia said. She went behind the blanket.

"Hurry up, my arms are getting tired," Zosia said. Katia shyly handed her mother the bottle. "Don't show anybody!"

"Thank you, darling. I'll just put this out here." She placed the bottle on a cart loaded with various suspicious-looking jars out in the corridor. "Let some doctor analyze it."

Marusia studied her daughter-in-law. Zosia had vomited a bit on the bus, but she seemed better. She certainly looked healthier than Yurko, whose hands shook each time he brought a cigarette to his lips.

Zosia stood up again. "I have to get us 'official,'" she said, and in her thick red shoes she sidestepped the hordes of people that barricaded her path to the nurse's desk.

"Hey, *medsestro*," she called out to the nurse.

"Are you number five? Let's see your number card."

"No, *we're* number five," shouted a tiny woman with a check coat holding an overstuffed shopping bag. "Me and my family here are all number five. See!" She thrust her card in front of the nurse's face and glared at Zosia.

"Fine," said the nurse. She wrote something down in her notebook and handed the woman another card.

"Go out to the corridor and down the stairs to the basement. Number six!"

"Excuse me," Zosia said to the nurse. "We were never given a number. Someone either stole our number or your incompetent staff didn't think we needed one."

"Then you can't be here. Go back outside and get in line for a number. Six! Number six!"

"You don't seem to understand." Zosia's voice was louder but very self-assured. "My husband was directly contaminated from the fires at Chornobyl. He was exposed to radiation. They made us come in here immediately because he needs emergency medical care. His condition is worse than anyone's here."

The nurse looked bored and annoyed at Zosia's high-handed speech. "Everybody has a number. You go out like you were supposed to and get one."

"But he was there when the fires started at the plant. He helped put the fires out. . . ."

"Number six!" the nurse shouted, wedging her hefty backside firmly against her chair.

Zosia wished she had something valuable to give the woman. She eyed and measured the nurse's feet beneath the desk, then took off one of her high-heeled shoes and held it up for the nurse to see. "Here. These must be worth something."

The nurse looked for a minute, then glanced back down at her notebook. She was waiting.

Zosia continued. "Look, you probably have a beautiful daughter who would love to wear these. Or for yourself. Why not! Or sell these on the black market for a real wage."

The nurse's pig eyes were greedy. "Put them under the desk," she mumbled.

"Not until my husband is given medical treatment first."

The nurse sighed heavily, then yawned without covering her mouth, exposing a wealth of gold and silver teeth.

"Wait. Here's one shoe." Zosia placed it beneath the desk. "You get the other one after he's taken care of."

The nurse admired a shrewd operator. "Good. I believe I called your number. Number six?" she said looking directly at Zosia.

Zosia smiled. She waved over her family while the nurse argued with a young couple who claimed they were the true holders of number six. "Impostors," the nurse spat out. "Who do you think you are—playing a game with me? Go outside and get another number card. You can't jump ahead of everybody. I can have you arrested for that!"

The couple, in their early twenties and young enough to have never experienced the authority of a big-city bureaucracy, were dumbfounded when the nurse took their card away. They left the room without any protest.

Marusia had kept a close watch on the scene and understood when Zosia motioned her to come up to the desk. The old woman helped Yurko stand up and steadied him. His arm rested heavily around her shoulders.

"Children, stay here and guard our things." She grasped him around his waist and lead him slowly across the room.

Zosia quickly took off her other shoe and held it tightly in the crook of her arm. She rushed to meet them and caught her husband just as his knees buckled. "I'm fine," he rasped.

"We're almost there, a few more steps, dear," Zosia said, eyeing the fat nurse who sat calmly watching them struggle.

Yurko's body was very hot, and his cotton shirt was soaked through. "This takes too much time," the nurse yelled. "Natalka!" she called to another nurse who leaned idly against a wall, talking to a man dressed in a filthy white duster.

"Natalka! Come here and bring that lazy idiot with you!" Natalka scowled back at the nurse. She and her companion were finishing a shared foreign cigarette.

"Take this man to ward four. Internal medicine."

"Come on *bratiku,*" the man in white said. He gruffly grabbed hold of Yurko, but Marusia would not loosen her grip around his waist.

"What are you waiting for?" said the nurse at the desk. "Get the wheelchair."

Natalka indolently shuffled to a wheelchair. In it sat an old man who hobbled out of the seat. "Now sit him down here," Natalka commanded Marusia. She was irri-

tated that she had to take charge of Yurko and was surly
to the old woman, who seemed to be afraid of her.

"He'll go straight to the ward, and you can go to
the basement where you'll be taken care of," the nurse at
the desk cut in.

"What about the rest of my family?" Zosia demanded. Her head itched from perspiration and her
stomach cramped. "I have two little children, and my
old mother-in-law here. What about them?"

The huge nurse smugly stared at Zosia. "They'll
just have to go outside and get their own number." Then
with a grunt she dismissed Zosia and Yurko and proceeded to call out more numbers.

Zosia refused to be put off. "Find a place for all of
us or you'll never get this other shoe," she said.

The nurse mumbled, "Either you give me that shoe
or your husband can rot on the floor."

Zosia's eyebrow twitched. She glanced at Yurko,
who sat uninvolved. She thought hard for a minute.

"*Mamo,* take this shoe. Stay here with the children
until I come back. I'm going with Yurko to make sure
he's all right."

"You're not allowed," Natalka sneered. Immediately Zosia knew that Yurko might well end up in a corridor all night, forgotten and neglected. She knew far
too well the taciturn laziness of workers like this Natalka
who resented fulfilling any given duty. It was like that in
every single job she ever had, even at Chornobyl. She
knew that Yurko could die while this slovenly bitch

flirted with her worthless boyfriend who had no intention of working if he could get away with avoiding it. And absolutely no one would be held responsible.

"I'm going! If you try to stop me, I'll push your ugly face so far into your fat *dupa* that you'll beg me to find a gun and shoot you," Zosia exploded. "Mama, I'm going with Yurko."

Marusia cried quietly to herself, nodded, and took a last mournful look at her son, who slumped in the wheelchair, his head hanging down. Then she retreated back to the children.

"Let's go," Zosia said to Natalka. She walked behind the wheelchair and Natalka's billowy rump, which swayed rhythmically like two large bells clanging together. Zosia didn't mind following in her nylon-stockinged feet. She almost enjoyed the soothing coolness of the linoleum floor on her tired soles. It took her mind off her nausea. A devil of a time to be pregnant, Zosia thought to herself.

Later, Zosia returned alone. Marusia and the children were sitting close together. Many more people had jammed into the room, all straining to hear their numbers called above the din. Still others were able to sleep despite the wretched stink of cigarettes and bodies reeking of fear and illness.

Marusia's tired face broke into relief when she saw Zosia. "How is he?" She asked worriedly. The children were asleep with their heads resting on rolled up sweaters.

"He's very ill," she said, not sure how much to tell Marusia. "When they saw him in the ward, they put him in a bed with an oxygen tent. There are a few others in his room who were infected by radiation. Like him."

Marusia nodded and understood. She was afraid to ask if he would live. "At least he'll have a bed to himself tonight, thank God." It was too soon to ask when he would be able to return home. Of course, Marusia thought, we can't leave until he does, but when? She decided that she would stay behind with Yurko no matter what, even if Zosia and the children returned to Starylis in a couple of days.

The same large nurse was still at her desk calling out the numbers that would lead the people on to the next phase of their wait. Zosia walked over to her and shoved the other shoe quickly beneath the desk.

The nurse acted as though nothing unusual was happening. "Take your family out to the corridor and down the stairs to the basement. All of you will be taken care of there." Then she stamped another official card for Zosia to take with her and looked away.

"Let's go, *Mamo,* before she changes her mind," Zosia said, gathering their belongings and grabbing the clumsy suitcase.

Before leaving the emergency room, Zosia couldn't help glancing back one more time at her beautiful lost red shoes—always the cause of trouble. Shoes that were given to her by a man who forced her a long time ago to become his lover. Otherwise, Yurko would have lost his high position at the plant. She demanded those shoes in payment and wore them with the pride of a war hero who displays his medals. Just as well that Yurko got some more use out of those damn things, Zosia thought.

She couldn't see the shoes because the nurse had already hidden the treasures beneath her own great toes, and Zosia was briefly reminded of a picture from a forbidden prayer book someone in her family had smuggled in from the West. It was a holy picture of the Virgin standing on top of a globe, with a crushed snake beneath her bare feet.

"I am going mad," she muttered to herself.

Chapter 8

THE ROOM IN the basement to which Marusia and her family were banished proved to be little better than the emergency room. But at least they were given two thin mattresses to share, along with stained, lumpy pillows and frayed blankets. They were also given two meals a day, sometimes three, though the food was paltry, mostly cold, hard potatoes with dry cucumber and tomato slices and a dollop of thick, pasty gray kasha. Meat was never part of the menu. Milk was given in tin cups for the children and weak black tea for the adults. Marusia's food from home was long gone.

A week had passed, and no authority figure had said anything about returning home.

Marusia tried to keep her emotions hidden because she was aware that Katia and Tarasyk became upset and sullen whenever she began to cry. Katia especially kept asking when they were going to go back to their home. She missed her dolls and the animals, especially her cat.

Tarasyk pouted more and was constantly wetting his pants. They hadn't, of course, brought enough clothing with them, and Tarasyk had developed a rash on his thighs. Marusia was grateful that he hardly complained, and that he slept a great deal, sometimes falling asleep in the middle of eating his dinner. He had to be coaxed into eating anything and usually sat morosely, clutching his worn-out stuffed rabbit to his chest, shaking his head in a fierce "no" to any comforting words Marusia or his mother uttered.

Marusia wasn't allowed to visit Yurko. Only one visitor was permitted each patient, and that right belonged to Zosia. When she felt abandoned by her daughter-in-law, and worn-out by the children's bad tempers, she consoled herself by searching the room for people she had known back in Starylis. She was sorry that Zosia had insisted they separate themselves from their own people and wait in a line for evacuees from some other, contaminated village. Perhaps her neighbors were in another part of the hospital or somewhere else altogether. Even so, Marusia reasoned, it was lucky in a way that they were in a hospital—Yurko would be properly looked after, and she was near enough to know how he was.

The windows were painted orange and locked securely shut. The basement stank of perspiration, baby diapers and foul odors from the hordes of unwashed and unhealthy people. By the fifth day, tempers flared and fights erupted because people were tired and frustrated and no one had bothered to examine them or soothe their ailments. The evacuees had expected to be packing up and boarding the buses back to their lives, and they became even more downcast as the successive days turned into successive evenings and they knew that they weren't going to leave, at least not that day. Perhaps tomorrow, they repeated to themselves every night.

"That's my dress! Give it back, you *svoloch!*" a woman screamed out. Marusia turned around and saw a short, black-haired woman ripping the front of a red and white polka-dot dress off another woman. The woman in the torn dress was taller and much heavier, and after a moment in which astonishment registered on her jowly face, she hit the smaller woman square on her jaw.

"Thatta girl, Liena. Give it to her good," shouted a thin man with a gray mustache.

"Mind your own business! That's my sister she's hitting," another dark-haired woman shouted at the man. She rushed up to the fallen victim. "Get a doctor! Is this supposed to be a hospital? Get some help."

The big woman stood over them, her arm raised over her head. Then she looked down and started to whine over her torn dress. "Look at what that whore did to me!"

Some of the men and young boys started to whistle and clap. The woman in the polka dots looked around and pressed the flap of the ripped piece over her exposed slip. She looked to her husband, who was suddenly embarrassed and turned his back on everyone. Another onlooker, a young woman, picked up her blanket and gently wrapped it around the woman's shoulders.

The dark-haired woman was on the floor, sitting up with her hand over her swollen face. She wailed at her sister, and the two of them crept off to another part of the room where several people searched in their belongings for pieces of *salo* that would help alleviate her bruises.

"How crazy we've become," said a skinny old woman with a bright paisley babushka. She dragged her thin mattress toward Marusia and Tarasyk, who had slept through the outburst. A trail of its down feathers fluttered out of a hole. "I don't want to wake him," she said in a hushed voice, but made a great noise when she plopped down the mattress. "Oh, how sweet your grandchildren are. I miss mine so much. Come here, darling," she said to Katia. "Here." She gave the little girl a sugar cube still in its wrapper.

"Katia, say thank you," Marusia coaxed. The little girl's lower lip puffed out, and she looked down at the sticky square in her hand.

"Never mind, *malen'ka,*" the skinny woman said. She reached out to Katia, saw that she was crying, and wiped her eyes with her thumbs. "She must be tired. It's so cramped for the children."

Marusia nodded. The women talked together for a bit in guarded tones, but gradually their stories of how they came to this place flowed out more freely. The woman said she was an evacuee from Prypiat' and was separated from her sons. She was a widow like Marusia and had three sons—all engineers—working at the plant. "I'm not sure where they are," she sighed. "I worry about them, and I miss my own grandchildren. But my brother and his wife are here." She pointed to a chunky man wearing a blue suit with Lenin medals covering its wide lapels. A dour brunette was seated next to him on their mattress. The sister-in-law was scratching her legs. "I want to get away from them," she whispered. "That Stefa's got some rash on her and my brother got it, and who knows how dangerous it is, so I want to keep away from them."

Marusia thought that was wise, although she knew how easy it would be to become infected by anyone in this place . . . people were packed too close together. How could you avoid someone coughing on your neck or breathing on your food? She overheard people around her complaining about their stinging eyes, and sore throats, and headaches. Older people, men mostly, coughed their phlegm onto the floor, which was yet to be washed. Cigarette smoke hung heavily in the air, and they all had to leave their waste in buckets that sat full and stinking for hours in the corridor before someone thought to collect them.

Marusia herself was feeling ill. She breathed heavily, broke into sweats often, and had coughing spells that went on for several minutes at a time, causing her to lose her breath whenever she had to get up from the mattress. One of her coughing spells came on while she was talking to her new friend, whose name was Marta Fedenko. "Oh, that sounds bad," said Marta. She took out a thermos from her plastic shopping bag. "Try this. Onion and honey in red wine. It might help."

Marusia took a cupful and drank it down. "Thank you." Her chest felt warm, and she liked the sweet silky taste of the clover honey on her tongue. "Are you a healer?" Marusia suddenly thought of Slavka Lazorska and once again felt a stab of homesickness.

"Oh, no," Marta Fedenko laughed. "I'm a *pensionerka*. But before that I used to be a seamstress."

"My son was stationed at Prypiat' when the fires started," Marusia said. Then she started to cry, because she was tired and ill and felt so alone. "My son is contaminated with radiation. He's in this hospital. I haven't seen him since the night we first came here."

"God grant that he will live," Marta Fedenko said, and kept silent, looking down politely so that Marusia could weep a bit.

After a while Marusia said, "I wish we could all go home and I could take him back with me and nurse him."

Katia listened closely to the old women's talk, then pouted and went back to playing with her doll. She pretended to feed it the sugar cube, but stopped when she saw that another little girl, with black braids, was watching her. She hid the cube in her dress pocket and ignored the girl. "Look," whispered the other girl. She held up a small chocolate duck that was half wrapped in torn colorful foil. "I got this." She pulled off its head and gave it to Katia. The head had melted and then hardened and reformed into an egg-shaped blob. Katia bit into the milk chocolate and smiled, and Marusia remembered that it was Easter Day.

THE EVENING MEAL was dispensed by two nurses who monitored a long table in the corridor. The evacuees were made to stand with their chipped plates and wait in long lines for stingy scoops of warmed-over food. Later, after the people had eaten hurriedly, rushed by the nurses who wanted the plates and utensils returned, a pall descended over the evacuees. In a far corner of the dank room, some of the men gathered and played cards. One man lulled his children with a mandolin and a soft voice. Women tidied up their small territories, ingeniously draping long scarves and skirts over the bare hanging lightbulbs to shield the light from their children's eyes as they tried to sleep. During the course of the night, old men rose and stumbled over the cramped bodies to relieve themselves in the pails; men and women lowered their voices and argued about what would happen next.

The room was still, and Marusia fell into a deep sleep. Since her arrival in Kyiv, she had dreamed often about the cow she left behind in her village. That night, the cow didn't appear. Instead, she saw herself walking in a fog toward the abandoned cowshed, where several mice were eating the hay. Marusia awoke with the certain knowledge that her beloved cow had died.

She sat up, wiped her eyes, coughed, and then looked around to see if she had disturbed anyone. Zosia was asleep on the other mattress with Katia cradled in her arms. Tarasyk was gone. She inched over to where Marta Fedenko lay across her thin mat, her scarf pulled low over her eyes to keep out the light. She was snoring, as were several other people surrounding the small space where Marusia and her family slept.

Marusia struggled to get up. She did not want to wake anyone. Her babushka had slipped off to her shoulders, and she felt the sting of electricity crackling over her thin, messy hair when she pulled the paisley woolen scarf back on her head. She stepped over the sleeping bodies and looked around the room in the dim light.

"Did you see a little boy with blond curly hair?" Marusia frantically whispered to a man propped up against a wall, smoking a cigarette.

He grunted an obscenity and turned away from her.

A woman's voice loudly ordered Marusia to shut up because she wanted to sleep. But another voice, also a woman's, coming from the same direction said kindly, "I saw some children go out into the corridor."

Marusia blindly thanked the second voice and hurried down the badly lit corridor. There was only one direction to go, and Marusia glanced into each of the tiny windows set in the doors to unknown rooms. She saw beds, and patients, and a group of doctors playing cards, but not Tarasyk.

She followed the L-shaped passage and heard high-pitched voices. A dog yelping. Marusia sighed out a loud "thank God" when she saw three children huddled around a small dog. She grabbed Tarasyk's hand.

"We saw the doggie, so we followed him," said the little dark-haired girl whom Marusia recognized as Katia's new friend.

The dog was mottled brown and black. Its fur was clotted with burrs, and its pink tongue hung limp from its mouth. It looked at the old woman with calm brown eyes and wagged its stub of a tail.

"Where did this dog come from?" Marusia asked.

"We saw him in the hall. He must be hungry. Then we chased him down here," said another girl.

"Tarasyk, why did you leave us?" Marusia scolded. Her grandson snatched his hand away, but she grabbed hold of it again.

"Let's go back, children," Marusia said. "Don't leave like that again. You'll worry your parents."

"What about the doggie?" the dark-haired girl asked.

"He'll go back where he came from," she said. "He has a home, too. He'll find his family. Now, let's go back and find your parents. Come on."

The children followed the old woman. They had little trouble finding their way back to their mattresses.

In her own area, Marusia tripped over Zosia's outstretched legs on the floor. She laid Tarasyk down on their mattress and let him snuggle into the crook of her arm. She peered into Zosia's face: Her mouth was wide open, her face relaxed. Good thing I'm still looking out for the children, she thought.

Somebody grumbled. Marusia propped herself on her elbow in time to see the dog being chased out of the room by an old man. "What a horrible place," she muttered. She settled herself and tried to catch some sleep before it was time to wake up and wait in line for another awful breakfast.

Tarasyk tossed his head and pushed himself away from Marusia. He rolled over on one side so that his back was pressed against her. I wish he wouldn't nap so much during the day, Marusia thought. Now he won't sleep. She reached out to stroke his head to soothe him. He didn't turn to her, and when she bent over to look at him, she noticed how tight his eyes were shut. She touched his hair again, and her fingers held a sprig of his blond curls. She looked closer and inspected his head to see if there were any lice or worms from that dog. She saw none, only small patches of reddish bald spots on the back of his head.

We have to leave here, Marusia vowed, or at least find a room with a real sink.

Chapter 9

ZOSIA WAS RESTLESS. Her bottle of perfume was almost empty. It was important to her that she splash just a drop on her temples and wrists; it helped her to survive the basement's stench.

Her temper was quick and harsh in the cold, over-crowded room with its sickening pea green walls. Thick water pipes hung so low from the ceiling that she bumped her arms whenever she stretched. It was too easy to get into arguments, especially with the children and her mother-in-law.

Whenever she felt closed in, she would steal away to take a look at Yurko, even though his deteriorating condition depressed her. She spent most days wandering around the hospital corridors.

Within a day after relinquishing her shoes, Zosia was able to trade her lipstick for another pair—flat black vinyl slip-ons with cheap rubber soles she wouldn't be caught dead in at work. She got them from a man whose wife was laid up in a ward like Yurko's. He thought the lipstick would cheer his wife up. The shoes were a bit large for her feet, and the soles were tearing apart at the toes, but she didn't mind as long as she was able to walk away from the misery of the basement room for a few hours every day.

It was well over a week after they'd been evacuated before the refugees were given ration coupons and six rubles per adult in compensation money. Zosia was determined to take her money and leave the hospital, at least for a day. Maybe she could find some drinking friends of one of her lovers. Someone like that might take her in, and then later, if she could talk someone into it or bribe somebody, they might let her family move in until they could all return to Starylis. She might even finagle a new bottle of perfume.

She felt guilt that stopped her short when she realized that Yurko was not included in her plans.

The corridors leading to Yurko's room were filthy even after the *babysi* slopped the floors with their bottomless buckets of dirty water and chlorine that was supposed to provide a veneer of sanitation. Zosia hated the sounds the women made when they sloshed their dark mops around the legs of Yurko's hospital bed. It was always the same. No change in his condition. No change in the smells of his room. No change in her sad life.

Zosia had trouble breathing. Her head ached more

than usual, and her throat was sore. She needed air. Yurko wouldn't notice. He was either asleep or completely listless whenever she came to see him. She'd see him later, when she came back.

The evacuees had been given strict orders never to go outside, because, as she overheard one disgruntled man repeat, they would "infect the city." Her anguish festered deep within her claustrophobia, until one afternoon she simply walked out the front doors with the authority of a regular city dweller in Kyiv—a doctor or nurse just off duty, ready to start her holiday, certainly not an evacuee. She pranced down the steps and into the street. At first her eyes smarted from the bright sunlight, but then they fixed hungrily on the fresh blooms of tulips and chestnut trees that brightened the dingy gray of the bulky concrete buildings.

Zosia knew Kyiv well. When she was a younger woman she had spent many weekends there in the company of small-time party officials who bribed her to come with them for a good time. She had been promised important jobs that turned out to be inconsequential, until she was transferred to Chornobyl. And what the hell good was that, she wondered. If I had been a *Kyivlianka* back then—in a real city where there were opportunities and people who liked me—I wouldn't be here now, like this, a hooligan and with a half-dead husband. . . .

She thought about her last lover at Chornobyl. Maybe he was also in Kyiv, forced to be just another refugee like her. Was he thinking of her? Was he sorry for the way he had treated her the last few times?

Hell no, she thought. He never wanted me, really. Now Yurko will be gone, too. . . . She cried openly for the first time since she'd left the village. It was refreshing to feel the soft spring breezes dry her wet cheeks.

Down the Khreshchatyk, Kyiv's main street, she paused in front of a large store window. On display was a female mannequin wearing a pink and green mohair skirt and matching jacket with a large red cloth string bag dangling from its upturned wrist. The dummy's blond wig was askew, and its high arched feet were shoeless. Zosia laughed.

"How are you, my friend?" she said softly. Back in the days when she was new to Kyiv, she used to stare at this very same dummy and admire some other ill-fitting outfit that it wore. "Stuck here too, darling," she said. "Girls like us never get anywhere."

She caught her own reflection in the window and decided she liked the way she looked; like Cleopatra, she thought.

She walked further down the street and saw how crowded the sidewalks suddenly were. Outdoor kiosks were open for business. She carefully counted out enough of her evacuation money to buy Marusia a plastic hair comb, since the old woman had complained only that morning about how snarly her hair had become. For the children she bought a bag of candy, the kind with sweet apple and cherry jam fillings. For her husband she bought a small bouquet of red and yellow tulips, though it seemed to her to be a stupid thing to get for someone who had never had much interest in such things.

More people positioned themselves on the side-walk. Old women were eagerly sweeping the wide street, and Zosia heard the faint trumpet blasts of a band. She poked her head between the bystanders and realized that a parade was about to come down the street.

The music grew louder and more familiar. She saw an orderly group of young children in white shirts with red neckerchiefs marching together—Young Pioneers, whose scrubbed little faces looked too serious to be children's. Two of them were holding a large banner with the words: SLAVA—GLORY and MAY DAY—MAY, 1986. The people on the sidewalks cheered and kept their applause steady when the Ukrainian troops of the Soviet Red Army marched ahead of the tanks and military warheads mounted on flatbed tractors. Another float carried a flo-ral copy of the Monument of the Motherland, better known as the Iron Maiden. Zosia had seen the original many times, a white metal monstrosity that stood high and ugly over the polluted Dnipro River. It was taller than the golden domes of St. Sofia, so that it would be—as someone once explained to Zosia a long time ago—more important than religion. Like the original, the floral statue wore a long Grecian toga, very like America's Statue of Liberty, except that the Iron Maiden held a sword and shield up to the sky, as though chal-lenging God to a duel.

Riding along with the floral Iron Maiden was a robust blond woman surrounded by her fourteen children. She had several medals pinned prominently on her huge chest. She stood as though at attention, never waving to the crowds. Her children stood silently by her, observing the people in mute contempt.

More bands played on, more young girls in colorful Ukrainian costumes marched to the music. They smiled and waved, and the red and yellow ribbons from the flower wreaths on their heads whipped high in the air behind them.

The old veterans marched next. Many were obviously sucking in their guts because their old war uniforms were stretched to the seams. Others marched in their best shiny blue suits, wearing all of their war medals on their lapels. Some of the old men were in wheelchairs, and many hobbled and staggered behind the rest. These were the war heroes who had saved the Motherland from fascism, and they received the loudest cheers and applause from the crowd.

Zosia felt dizzy and clammy. She accidentally bumped into a television cameraman, who yelled at her to stay behind the rope barrier.

She wanted desperately to get away from the crowds. She pushed her way out of the tight clusters of parade watchers and walked up the Khreshchatyk, then away from the main street, turning at a corner she vaguely remembered, near the Kyiv State University. She sat on a bench in the park across the street from the red university building. There she dropped her heavy head between her legs and waited for the nausea to pass. After a bit, the breeze kicked up the fragrance of roses and revived her.

Too bad the children didn't see the parade, she thought. They would have liked it. They would have liked this park, too. She stared at a woman selling ice cream.

She sucked on one of the overly sweet hard candies she had bought and felt better. Then she spotted the glass display cases where copies of the daily paper, *Pravda,* were hung for anyone to read. She went over to the glass plates that protected the pages and searched for anything about Chornobyl—perhaps things were back to normal there and they could return. But all she found was a tiny paragraph on one of the last pages that simply stated there had been a small radiation "eruption" at the nuclear power plant, and that the good citizens had nothing to worry about.

Well then, she thought. If there was nothing to worry about, and if the city's children were marching in the May Day parade, and the people of Kyiv were not in the least bit alarmed about anything, then things are fine after all. Pretty soon they'll let us go home.

Why not now, she thought. Maybe I should just go right now to the train station, get a ticket, and get the children, maybe Yurko too, and leave. No, I'll get Yurko later, when he's better. I can at least get tickets for the children. Marusia, too.

Zosia felt very proud of herself for her logic. If trains were running to Chornobyl, she reasoned, then it was all right to go home. They'll tell me for sure at the train station.

She paid her *kopiika* for the Metro and held on to the escalator that took her down the long, long descent into the cavernous subway tunnels. The children—it's for them, she reasoned. Katia had a little diarrhea last night, and Tarasyk has that rash and probably lice in his hair, no wonder some of it is falling out. . . .

The subway wasn't crowded. She was happy to get a seat. I can visit Yurko on the weekends—with Marusia. Or maybe we can transfer him to a hospital nearer to home . . . maybe in Prypiat'. Or if we leave him, well, it's only a couple of hours or so by train to Kyiv. Yurko would understand. She pressed the bag filled with candy and Marusia's comb closer to her chest, and then realized that she had dropped Yurko's flowers behind somewhere.

At the railroad station, Zosia was unprepared to see the mobs of mostly women and children waiting in long lines.

"What's going on here?" Zosia asked a woman in Russian. The woman was holding the hand of a little girl dressed in a frilly dress and with white ribbons in her braided hair.

"I'm trying to get my child on a train to Moscow. Or somewhere . . ."

"What for? Why?"

The woman turned her attention to her child, who was complaining that she was tired.

"Excuse me," Zosia said, "but is it summertime vacation already?" She knew that Russians in Ukraine liked to start their vacations sooner than anyone else.

"No, of course not," the woman said in annoyance. "Haven't you heard anything? About the accident?"

"At Chernobyl," the little girl cut in. "Don't be an idiot."

The mother ignored the child's rudeness. "So much radiation there. It's awful."

Zosia was alarmed. "What do you mean, please?"

"So much radiation. An explosion . . ."

"Did you come from the moon?" the child said in exasperation.

Her mother smiled. "Yes, it's true. Radiation is polluting Kiev. We've known it for days. That's why we're sending our children to Moscow where they'll be safer. I've got an official letter myself."

Zosia felt numb and confused and not sure how much to trust this Russian woman. "But so many children were marching just now in the May Day parade."

"Not me," the little girl said with pride. "Just the stupid *khakhly*. Not us."

"Yes, that's right darling," the woman said distantly. Then she eyed Zosia. "*Tovarishch*, where are your children?"

"Oh, back at home," Zosia said. She moved away from them and reckoned that there were about eighty people ahead of her. "How much is a ticket?"

"Three rubles, but who knows for sure," said another woman. "That's high, and they keep changing the price. At least the children will be safe. Whatever it costs, we mothers will pay."

"Why is that?" Zosia heard her voice tremble with anger.

"Because the government won't say that there's anything wrong."

"That's so we don't panic," piped in another woman in front of them.

The first woman Zosia had spoken to said, "I know it's worth it for my Tamara here." She looked down lovingly at the little girl, who ignored her and pretended to be interested in something invisible on the ground.

Zosia didn't have enough money—she had spent it on her gifts. She was sorry she had bought the things at the kiosk—she had eaten too much of the candy, and the flowers were lost, and the stupid comb for Marusia was unnecessary because she wouldn't use it anyway. She had forgotten all about buying herself perfume.

Zosia walked out and found the bus that would take her back to the hospital. "Bastards!" she kept murmuring under her breath. People heard her on the bus, but they ignored her as though she were just another drunk, or worse, just another crazy, angry woman cheated by an unfaithful lover.

"WHERE HAVE YOU been! Why didn't you tell me you were going?" Marusia was scolding Zosia. "*Hospody*, I thought they took you away too!"

Zosia ignored Marusia's wails and gave the children the bag of candy. Katia was delighted and stuck several pieces in her mouth at once. Tarasyk was uninterested and silently watched his sister's cheeks balloon with the sweets.

"*Mamo*, listen to me," Zosia whispered. Her voice was so low the old woman had to bend down to hear her better. "I was outside in the city. We're not safe here either. People are leaving Kyiv."

"What are you talking about?"

"I saw it all. I was at the train station. Hundreds of children are getting out of here because of the radiation. It's worse than anyone thought. We can't stay here either. We'll all die here just as we would back in Starylis."

"*Maty Bozho!*" the old woman exclaimed. Then she whispered, "Where would we go?"

Zosia looked behind her and noticed that Marta Fedenko was listening to their conversation. She moved closer to her mother-in-law and whispered in her ear, "Moscow. Or maybe to Siberia, to my mother."

"No, not there." Marusia shook her head. She had always been afraid of Siberia because of rumors she heard of labor camps and jails filled with sinful people. "The children can't go there."

"It's better there. Safer."

Marusia firmly shook her head. "No. Not Siberia." She had always suspected that Zosia's family were convicts. "No. Moscow is better."

"Only the children can go," Zosia said. "We don't have the money for all of us."

Marusia pursed her lips and didn't say anything more. She didn't like this plan because she hated to think of Katia and Tarasyk, so little, traveling all that way like that. Who would care about them? She shook her head again. "No. They can't go alone."

"I can't afford a ticket for the children and both of us," she repeated.

"And Yurko," Marusia said gently.

"Yes, naturally, but he's so ill. . . . Are we going to wait until he's better? When will that be?"

Marusia saw things clearly. She looked at Zosia's worn, sallow face and felt sorry for her. She loved her grandchildren, but Zosia was their mother after all. And *she* was Yurko's mother. It was very clear to her what must be done. "You go with the children," she said. "You know how to get them around the city, and you'll get them there safely. I'm too old and scared to go on there. You take my compensation money and use it for the trip.

I'll stay here with Yurko. I'm already used to how things are around this place. I'll wait until he's well, then we'll return back home. That's all. It's easy."

Zosia gazed at her mother-in-law with softness. "That's the best idea. Naturally, that's the only normal thing to do. Of course!"

Chapter 10

THE NEXT MORNING, Zosia went as usual to visit her husband. As always, she sat in a chair near his bed, watching him sleep. Sometimes she could help him eat some greasy soup or whatever she'd been able to take from her own dinners. Now she wasn't sure whether to tell him anything of her plan to leave that night. There didn't seem to be any reason to tell him anything.

She waited several minutes for the nurse to take away his bedpan. Yurko wheezed into a coughing fit, then finally settled back on his pillow, his mouth open, saliva dripping down his chin. Zosia had to pull her chair closer to see his face behind the plastic oxygen tent clouded by his coughs.

"You the wife?" the nurse asked Zosia. She was new. Zosia had never seen her before. She probably wasn't even aware that Yurko was contaminated from the zone.

"Pneumonia. Looks pretty bad." She clicked her tongue. "It might be worse. He'll be going to the X-ray division. It might be a lot worse than we think."

Zosia wanted to laugh. What a fool, she thought. The nurse kept clicking her tongue like the old women in Starylis did whenever they disapproved of something but were too guarded to give voice to their resentment. Zosia waited for her to go bother another patient.

"Yes, X-rays are what I need," Yurko said. His voice was so thin it was almost like a child's. He opened his eyes. "Smile, Zosen'ka. It's a joke."

Zosia saw how his face had shriveled and hung on his skull. She started to cry.

"Bad joke?" He half coughed and laughed at the same time. "Are you crying for me?"

"I'm so sorry, Yurochko. About everything. I wish our past was different."

He waved his bony, chapped hand. "It doesn't matter."

Zosia couldn't stop the flow of her tears because she was always hurting him, even at this moment when she believed he knew the emptiness of her feelings for him.

"The children miss you," she said. "And Mama, too."

He nodded. She always told him the same things.

"Yurko, listen. I'm taking the children to Moscow." She tried to keep her voice low and calm. "Mama agrees this is the best thing. It's bad in Kyiv for the children. They'll get sick."

He pointed a crusty finger at his chest.

"Well, maybe not like what you have. But it's better if we leave Kyiv. Your mother will stay here with you. Then we'll all come back home to Starylis."

He pointed a finger at her. "You too?"

"Yes! I always come back."

He didn't answer her.

"Time's up," the silly nurse chirped to Zosia before passing to another bed.

"Not me," Yurko whispered. "This time, I am leaving you."

"Yes, you too," Zosia said. "You'll come back!"

His throat gurgled a laugh. Liar, it mocked her.

ZOSIA WAS PLANNING to take the children out of the hospital early in the morning, before dawn. She knew that the night nurse would be asleep and no one would notice them going. She acted as though nothing unusual was going to occur. She didn't tell the children because she couldn't risk their telling another child about their plan, especially Katia. Word would get out, and then what next? Prison?

Zosia decided not to eat her dinner but to hoard it all in her shopping bag. Marusia did the same. Zosia knew that the cold overbaked potatoes and sour kasha would save them from hunger on their long day ahead. She wanted to get to the train station before it opened and get her place in line.

Marusia held Tarasyk in her arms that night. She

couldn't sleep, knowing that her grandchildren would be gone in a few hours. She gently stroked his head with the comb Zosia bought her, checking to see if more of his hair was falling out. She took the clumps from the comb's teeth and hid them in her dress pocket.

Zosia also inspected the back of his head. It looked worse, with more bald patches and his scalp ringed with an ominous shade of crimson. "Children get this in crowded situations," Marta Fedenko volunteered after she observed Zosia's concerned face. Zosia ignored the old woman.

"Mama look how sick they are," she said. "Tarasyk's hair. Now Katia is scratching her legs so much she's bleeding. This is awful!"

"Just like my sister-in-law," Marta Fedenko said.

"Maybe we got it from your family," Zosia snapped.

"*I* keep myself clean," the old woman retorted, then proceeded to move her mattress further away from Zosia.

"Good riddance," Zosia said. "Nosy old witch."

Marusia was upset. She liked talking to Marta Fedenko, and now just because Zosia was feeling mean or bad about things, why did she always have to take it out on others? And how many times had Zosia deserted her and left her to deal with the whiny children? At least Marta Fedenko tried to help her. Marusia thought of ways she could be nice to her after Zosia and the children had left, but that would come very soon, and she felt her chest ache again with fear and loneliness.

That evening, two men, drunk on vodka, got into a fistfight. Several of their friends and their women got involved. The commotion made everyone more jittery and harder to calm down for sleep. But at three in the morning, when Zosia touched Marusia's shoulder, she was amazed at how still and quiet the room was.

Marusia insisted on carrying Tarasyk. Zosia woke Katia and helped her stand up.

"We have to go, darling."

"To see *Tato?*" she whimpered.

"*Ssh,* yes, later. But here, put on your sweater. It'll be cold out."

"Can we go home?" She smiled for the first time.

"Yes, dear. But to a better place. Be quiet and tiptoe over the sleeping people. Don't wake them up."

The four of them escaped the basement room and hurried into the corridor and up a back staircase to another corridor that brought them to an entranceway.

"Hey, you! Where are you all going?" It was the shrill voice of a cleaning woman.

They stopped. Zosia turned and waited for the woman to approach her. "Who wants to know?"

The woman was short, with a snub nose, and her green lizard eyes darted from Zosia's face to Marusia's. "I can report you," she threatened. "No one is supposed to leave here without permission."

"Listen, you see this woman?" Zosia nodded toward Marusia. "She had just suffered a loss. Her husband, Colonel Makrenko, just died. That's right. Now she must return to her *dacha* because there will be several important people coming around to pay their respects to her. We've been at the colonel's bedside for three days now, and she must get her rest. They told us to go out through here, because of the Chernobyl people in our way."

"How do you know about Chernobyl?"

"Who do you think ordered the evacuation in the first place? The colonel!"

Marusia was too afraid to say anything. How could Zosia think up such an incredible lie? And yet people did what she wanted. Even if they didn't believe her, they seemed frightened and unsure enough not to take a chance in making her angry.

Zosia stared the cleaning woman down. "Anything else you need to know? Good. Now let the colonel's wife grieve in peace!"

The little woman stepped aside to let them pass. She pressed her mop down on the floor, but Marusia saw that she stared angrily at Zosia's back before swishing the mop's slimy tentacles against the floor.

Outside, the air was crisp but stank of diesel from the buses pulling into the parking lot. "I think those are more evacuees," Zosia said. "Wouldn't surprise me!"

They went in the opposite direction of the buses, near the parking lot floodlights. "So, the Metro's there. We can catch it. It's a short walk, we'll be fine," Zosia said. She took Tarasyk from Marusia's arms. "Wake up, darling. We're going for a nice walk."

"Good-bye, my beautiful ones," Marusia said, and hugged Tarasyk, then Katia, who pulled back. "You're not coming too, *Babo?*"

"No, sweetheart. I'll see you later. Back home." She kissed the little girl hard on both her cheeks, then she kissed Tarasyk the same way and made the sign of the cross over both of them.

"Bless you and may God watch over you," Marusia said, blessing Zosia. They hugged before she remembered that she was wearing her gold medallion with the Blessed Virgin imprinted on both sides. "Take it, it's pure gold. You can sell it if you have to. But it will protect you. Take this, too," Marusia said, pulling out a small embroidered pillow from her shopping bag, which she'd taken from home on impulse. "Sell this to a foreigner . . . American or German. Someone rich. They have money."

"Thank you. Take care of Yurko."

"I will. Write to me here at the hospital or back in Starylis. I'll be waiting for you."

They hugged again, and cried, and Marusia watched them until she could no longer see their silhouettes outlined against the glow of the harsh purple lights.

AT THE HOSPITAL entrance, more evacuees waited in line. Marusia stood with them and didn't return to her mattress in the basement until lunchtime the next day.

"Where were you?" Marta Fedenko demanded. "Where are your grandchildren?"

"A long story," Marusia said. She had waited in line all night and registered as a new evacuee. She showed them her internal passport stating that she had come from the radiation zone, and they gave her a new blanket and pillow and six more rubles.

Marta Fedenko handed Marusia her big suitcase. "I kept a watch over your things."

Marusia took it by the handle and swung it gently. "Oh, how light this feels. So empty, and light like air."

PART II

The Sky Unwashed

Chapter 11

Y URKO DIED ALMOST six months after the evacuation. All that time, Marusia had never given up her faith that Yurko would get better. That she would witness her son's death from the fallout in an alien city where doctors would refuse to listen to her or quell her worries was inconceivable. But in his last days she sat near her son's bed, alert, finally ready for a death watch. She prayed and hoped for a quick, merciful end. Though the doctors had promised to send him to a better hospital in Moscow, in fact they had simply let him waste away in his starched bed, his skin patched and crusty like dried brown leaves as his body neared death. He was forty-two years old, but when she looked at him for the last time through the oxygen tent, she saw the pinched-faced boy who used to catch toads and trout from the Prypiat' River in a time before anyone could have imagined the evil pollutants Chornobyl would blast forth.

Marusia tried to touch her son's hands through the plastic, alerting the nurses who hardly noticed his moans for water. They rushed to come and tell her to go away. Their voices behind their paper-thin surgical masks were harsh, and they laughed at her when she asked if he couldn't return with her to be buried back home in Starylis. "Are you crazy, *Baba?*" they chortled. "We'll have to burn this one." They whisked his body away, and Marusia's eyes stung from the antiseptic they poured over the floor where his bed had stood. No one spoke to comfort her. She heard only the lull of her own murmuring voice chanting prayers of mourning for his soul.

The bitter months had passed slowly for Marusia after Zosia and the children left for Moscow. Some of the other refugees were sent to sleep their last days on hospital beds. Others, like her friend Marta Fedenko, found relatives to take them in. The rest were sent to other refugee areas. Marusia stayed on until Yurko's death. After that, she was able to get another fifteen rubles from the government—"*nagrop,* coffin money," she heard the other refugees say when they got their paltry compensations. Hardly enough to live on, especially in a large city like Kyiv. She knew that sooner or later she would no longer be allowed to live at the hospital. She spent many wasted hours at various government offices futilely seeking permission to live in an apartment in Kyiv. The time came when she finally realized she had nowhere to go except home. When she could get hold of them, she eagerly read both the Russian and Ukrainian newspapers. Like all Ukrainians living in Soviet times, she had had to learn Russian, and from the papers she found that the fires at Chornobyl were over and that trains traveled there. She decided it must not be so bad anymore, not like the time when Zosia had tried to leave Kyiv. There was no question in Marusia's mind that she should return home.

Thanks to Marta Fedenko's relatives, who pulled a few bureaucratic strings in exchange for a percentage of her meager wages, she was, during her additional six months in Kyiv, able now and then to find work as a street sweeper. The job forced her to become familiar with the vast city, and soon she was resourceful enough to find and collect numerous empty vodka bottles to cash in for extra *kopiiky*. At the hospital, where she still claimed a mattress on the basement floor, she scavenged for discarded things that she could sell on the black market for real money in case she had to bribe the ticket agent at the train station to allow her to go to Chornobyl. She found many valuable items—half-bottles of aspirin, a man's jacket made of chapped greasy brown leather, a transistor radio with dying batteries—and sold them to surly young men at the huge Sunday morning bazaars held on the Plaza of the October Revolution, not so far from the hospital.

Marusia believed Zosia might return to the hospital, and so she needed to leave a message for her. On the back of an expired ration coupon she wrote, "Zosen'ka, I have gone back to our home in Starylis. Yurko has gone to the Lord. They have taken his body to be burned. There was nothing for me to do. Come home to me with the children."

She distrusted the nurses after the way they had treated her and her son. She had her eye on an old cleaning woman who had now and then offered sympathies during the long nights she had kept watch while Yurko's condition worsened. When the time came, Marusia gave the cleaning woman two of her precious rubles to get her promise that she would deliver the message to Zosia, should she ever come. With the rest of her money, Marusia parceled out enough for a train fare, third-class, to Chornobyl.

The town of Chornobyl was barely one hundred thirty kilometers north of Kyiv. On the train, Marusia was one of only four people in her car. The others were men very like the sullen workers she used to see back in Starylis waiting for the bus that took them to their jobs at the plant. The men ignored her when she greeted them. And they hardly spoke among themselves, but sat there, passively hunched over their meager breakfasts of black bread, tomatoes, *salo* and a bottle of vodka they passed to one another. She was hungry, but meant to save her lunch of bread and tomatoes for later.

The train pulled into the Chornobyl station at six o'clock in the morning, and Marusia walked the five kilometers miles from the station to the silent town. In the distance, she could make out the blinking red lights atop the antennas and chimney stacks of the plant building.

At the town's entrance, she stopped to look up at the huge, gaudy brick mural, with a metal relief of the Chornobyl nuclear power plant's skyline set beneath a metal sun holding a hammer and sickle. The word *Chornobyl* was spelled in bold Cyrillic letters.

Just as she reached the town's center, a garbled recording of the "Internationale" blasted from the loudspeakers perched on the lampposts. After the anthem, a woman's sweet voice came on to announce the day's bus schedules to the plant. She ended her announcements with a list of the workers who had been given job promotions. Then, several buses pulled up, and Marusia watched people emerge from the dingy gray apartment buildings. Marusia couldn't tell if they were men or women because all of them wore the same dark blue jumpsuits, knee-high rubber boots and felt berets. They also wore protective surgical masks dangling around their necks as though there were no compelling reason to use them. The workers boarded the buses that would take them to the plant in time for the morning shift, and would, Marusia knew, transport them back home. A new load of blue uniforms would take their places during the night.

"Hey, you! Chauffeur!" she yelled at the startled bus driver. "Hey, I need a ride to Starylis!"

The driver shook his head. "Starylis? Are you crazy, *Babo?* Nobody goes there anymore. Go away!"

"I'll pay," Marusia persisted. She heaved her heavy body up a step and barricaded the doors so that no one could pass her.

"You're crazy. Get out! Hey, *robitnyky!*" the driver yelled to the workers waiting behind Marusia. "Come on, we're late. Hop in. Not you, *babo!*" The workers pushed Marusia aside as they piled into the bus before the doors closed and it pulled away.

Marusia proceeded to walk the length of the town and past its borders, where she came upon another ugly brick mural that said, LEAVING CHORNOBYL—HAVE A GOOD TRIP! Marusia laughed bitterly. "Take your buses and go straight to the devil," she yelled back at the town. She spat on the soil behind her.

She found the redbrick path that led home. It was pockmarked with loose gravel, and weeds grew between the bricks. Marusia hobbled and felt her thick ankles giving way. After a while, she had to stop and take off her boxy, black plastic shoes. She had bought them in Kyiv just before she left, and already they were falling apart; the heel was coming unglued from the sole, and the cardboard instep was in shreds. She took off her black woolen stockings, studied her feet, and saw that her left foot was particularly swollen and that the corns between two toes were inflamed.

"*Do bisa,*" she cursed, wondering if she should leave off her stockings, which were already snagged from the bramble bushes she passed. She spotted some moss and milkweed growing near the side of the road and stuffed some of the soft greenery into her shoes. That done, Marusia was able to walk the rest of the eight kilometers to Starylis, stopping only once to drink some water from a stream, which she spat out because it tasted like coins.

Toward midmorning the wind picked up a bit, and the sun hid behind the charcoal clouds. Some of the dirt from the ground swirled in the breeze and sprinkled into Marusia's eyes and lips. Well, it's my own earth, she thought. I'm almost home now. She liked the taste of the dirt on her tongue, the rich grains of soil she wanted to believe were the same as before the fires. She tried not to think that maybe her house was somehow blown up by that "damned *radiatsia,*" whatever that was supposed to be. Like everyone else who had homes in the Chornobyl zone, Marusia had been obliged in the past to attend seminars at the *kolhosp,* where she had worked before her official retirement, about atoms and nuclear fission and energy, but she never really understood what it was all about. In her mind, the Trinity made more sense than what was being done at Chornobyl. Anyway, it was well over a year after the accident, Marusia reasoned. Surely the poison had disappeared by now. Even earthquakes, forest fires and blizzards have their ends after they do their damage.

The brick road had ended a kilometer back, and Starylis was just around the river bend. Marusia walked on the muddy dirt road that split through the woods and led her to the main highway, straight into the village center. She was hoping that a familiar car could pass her by, maybe a neighbor or a policeman would give her a lift home and tell her about what had happened to everyone after she had gone.

But there were no cars and no people. Marusia didn't hear any blue jays or woodpeckers. She listened in vain for a howling dog or a cow lowing to her calf. It was quiet.

In the village center, the post office was the first building on her way. The door was unlocked and squeaked open easily as she pushed it. On the dusty floor stood three huge overflowing sacks of mail. One of the sacks was untied, and Marusia reached in eagerly and grabbed a bundle of letters. They were postmarked a few days after the explosion. Nothing was sorted, nothing was delivered, no one had come to pick up or inquire about their letters and packages. She wondered if there was a letter to her; maybe Zosia had written about the children. But she was too disheartened to think of digging into the three lumpy canvas sacks. In the handful of letters she held, she recognized many of the names on the envelopes—neighbors and friends whom she had last seen so long ago. Where were they now, she wondered. She put back the letters from Odesa and Moscow and the birthday greetings written on the backs of colorful postcards with the usual bright reproductions of watercolors of flowers in elaborate vases.

The abandoned post office made her feel uneasy.

It's like ghost fingers tickling my neck, she thought. She left hurriedly and headed toward the village store. The torn screen door hung on its jamb and rattled when she pulled it open. Inside, the shelves were empty except for a half-opened can of dried-up paté and an old potato with sprouted shoots that had turned a crispy brown. Marusia noticed that no flies buzzed around the paté or the potato. Before she left, she spotted two unopened cans of black tea, which she remembered had always been there on the third shelf and were probably as old as herself.

Across the street from the store, Marusia saw that the *klub*, the village social center, was boarded up. Someone had spray-painted a skull and crossbones on the side of the building. Marusia found herself remembering the wedding reception of Evdokia's granddaughter, Hanna Koval, the little flirt who had had to get married. Yurko, poor unlucky Yurko, had danced with her more often than he should have. Then Zosia had caused such a scene about it! Everybody at the reception made jokes about Zosia's jealous behavior. Yurko and Zosia were always fighting about something stupid, and now it was too late for them to make it up. Marusia's stomach knotted. Zosia! Brave, mean-tempered, high-spirited girl! Where was she now? And the beautiful children?

She wiped her eyes and continued her way out of the village center and toward the familiar dirt road that led to her house. On the way, Marusia decided to stop at the home of her friends, the Metrenkos, who lived in the oldest and most traditional peasant-style *izba* house in Starylis. Ivan Ivanovich was the village clerk, and if he was home he would certainly have news about everyone. Marusia had always admired the gingerbread moldings that surrounded the windows and door of the old house. They were so classy, she thought. Ringing the bell, she called out, "Ivan Ivanovich, are you there?" and turned the brass knob. The door was unlocked. She gasped and coughed from the dust that drifted around her. The big old-fashioned brown-tiled stove was caked in soot, and piles of dishes and pots stood unwashed and crusty in the sink. The beds were unmade, and the linen was yellowed from the grime and sunlight. The closets were empty, and the beautiful carved oak kitchen table and chairs that Marusia had always coveted were gone. A patchy red and blue area rug remained on the floor, tufts of dog hair and dustballs almost hiding its floral pattern. An icon of the Madonna and Child still hung in a corner, except that the ruby and turquoise stones that were inlaid into the gilt frame were missing. Marusia picked up a hand-embroidered flaxen towel from off the floor. The towel was soiled with a footprint mark, and she tried to rub off the stain with her fingers. She draped it gently over the icon and made the sign of the cross before she left. The last thing she saw was a calendar with a picture of a young man singing, kissing into a microphone—it must have belonged to Marta, the Metrenkos' teenage daughter. The calendar was turned to April 1986, and

Marusia read a message scribbled in purple ink near the singer's photo that said, "Back soon."

Marusia's house was a few yards down the road from the Metrenko home. She walked more slowly than she had before. On the way, she noticed that many of her neighbors had left their laundry out to dry—clothing stiff now like petrified corpses swinging from a hangman's rope. She was terrified of seeing her home in ruins and felt her breath shorten with panic the closer she came to her house.

She looked anxiously for signs of life in all the houses she passed—a smoking chimney, the buzz of a saw cutting firewood for the winter, the motor of a threshing machine on the collective farm. But nothing.

Marusia took the path directly to her own gate. She sank to her knees on the ground, and she made the sign of the cross. She uttered a prayer of thanks to be back on the land where her mother and grandmother had lived. She was weak from hunger and from the long walk, and she worried over the unfamiliar aches she had felt festering in her body ever since she'd been forced to leave. Above all, she was sick from the cloud of loneliness that was choking her. She wailed and continued genuflecting. But her house was still standing, and even though she knew that somehow God had cursed her land, she grabbed a handful of soil and kissed it and rubbed it over her hands and face. She stood up and stared hard at every broken shutter, every crack in the windows and steps, before deciding to go in.

Luckily, no one had bothered to board up her house. Marusia detached the house key from the string she wore around her neck, timidly unlocked and opened her own door, and peered in. It had not been vandalized. Only mildew assaulted her nostrils. She noticed a few piles of hardened mouse droppings on the kitchen table and on the pantry shelves. But everything else seemed to be there—her few meager chairs, the kitchen table, the beds and feather-down comforters, the kilims on the wall—all there just as she had left them. Her own icon of the Madonna and Child was still nailed on her bedroom wall. She found matches and lit the votive candle on the small shelf beneath the icon and whispered another prayer.

The next thing she did was to start a fire in her woodstove as a signal of her arrival in case anyone was around. In her kitchen, she found the hand ax that hung on a wall, judged its sharpness with a caress of her thumb, and then chopped some of the birch logs that were piled near the stove for kindling. She dropped it all on top of the old white ashes inside the stove, lit a small sheet of leftover birch bark, which she placed under the kindling, and watched the hot blue flames wrap around the wood chips before she threw on the larger logs. The wood was dry enough and the logs' pungent odor was comforting because it erased the dank smell of the abandoned rooms.

Marusia then tested the faucets and was surprised when a thick stream of brown liquid rust emerged at first. Then clearer water flowed, but it was still tinged with rust and had a foul smell. She decided that from then on, she would boil the water before drinking it or cooking anything. Marusia went down into the root cellar and almost wept with gratitude when she found the hoarded jars of pickled tomatoes, beets and onions and the several other fruits and vegetables she had canned before—all untouched and waiting for her.

Marusia thought now how busy she would be cleaning the stench from her neglected house, making a new life for herself without her son and his wife and the grandchildren. She would live in her house until it was time for her to be buried in the graveyard down the road. Nothing would ever force her to leave Starylis again—not even another nuclear blast. She would die where she lived or be blown up with it.

Then she thought about her son, whose body was burned away into particles and without a decent burial. "I wished I could've brought him back with me," she sobbed to herself as she stoked the woodstove with a crowbar. "I could've nursed him back to health here, or at least have buried him." She cried long and hard and allowed herself the luxury of her tears for him. "As God wills," she declared several times out loud. She sighed and felt the weariness settle in her body.

She wiped her eyes with the backs of her sleeves, and remembered her favorite black gum that she had hidden in a glass jar in the back of her bedroom closet. It was still there—a black rubbery residue from the time she had made rope from hemp a few summers back. She scraped off a wad with an old butter knife and chewed it. The gum soothed her in a mellower way than the *samohon* she was used to drinking, and gradually she began to feel better.

Marusia went outside to inspect her little garden in the back of her house. She paused in front of the tiny empty shed where her beloved cow had lived. Marusia always regretted leaving the cow, and now she would never know what had happened to it or to its calf.

Her thoughts turned from the past to the long winter ahead. She wished she had left Kyiv earlier in the spring, in time to have planted more vegetables. Now it was far too late in the summer to sow anything plentiful. "Well, maybe there'll be some potatoes left in the fall. And I'll be ready for next spring!" she said out loud.

She gazed beyond her yard and saw the coppery-golden dome of the village church. "Tomorrow, I'll go there and ring the bells myself. Someone will hear that. I will ring them every day and they'll know that I'm back." Marusia felt satisfied.

She swatted her face and then spotted a tiny butterfly with translucent white wings landing feebly on a bush. She picked it up and saw that it was dying while it fluttered its white wings against the palms of her hands. Marusia saw that both of its antennae were crooked. She saw another one settle on a bush, and another one flitted around its twin. All of the butterflies had crooked antennae. "Devil's work!" Marusia yelled. She threw the dead butterfly on the ground and stomped it with her foot. She spat on it. "Devil's work!"

She scuttled into her house and slammed and bolted her door. Inside, Marusia gathered a handful of old herbs that she had dried on the ceiling beam in her kitchen—sage and parsley—and she hurled the tiny leaves into the stove.

She opened the door of her warm refrigerator— the stench made her cough. I have to get it, she said to herself. She searched the shelves for a vial of holy water from the last Epiphany she had celebrated in Starylis. She took it as a miracle that the water was well corked and had no offensive smell. It looked normal. She sprinkled all of the rooms. "Get out of my house you *zlyi dukh,* you bad spirit, who lived on my land while I was suffering so far away from home." She ran out and sprinkled some of the water over the overgrown garden and where she had seen the butterflies. "Get out! Get out!"

As exhausted and weary as she was, Marusia was unable to sleep her first night back. She watched the dancing flames of her stove diminish into hot red coals. She stoked the coals all night long and sat near her window waiting until the sun arose.

Finally, when the first pink of the early morning sky crept toward her line of vision, Marusia was relieved. "As long as the sun returns, I'll be all right. As long as the sun obeys God, then it isn't the end of the world." She felt refreshed and strong as she whispered her morning devotions in front of the window. When she was finished, she decided to celebrate her return home with half a cupful of the instant chicory coffee that she had carried with her all the way from Kyiv, and before beginning her new day's work, a fifty-gram shot of *samohon* that she had kept hidden in her kitchen.

Chapter 12

THE FIRST TIME Marusia took the lonely path toward the church, she was very afraid of what she might find. She imagined that all of the icons of the rapturous saints bedecked in their rich robes, always forgiving the earthly sinners with their mute eyes, might be replaced by skeletons of death. She looked up at the tower and saw that the two bells still hung in their tower.

She knocked on the doors and then found they were unlocked. She stepped into the dark building. The familiar scent of old beeswax candles and frankincense reassured her. The sanctuary was cool except for the unexpected warmth emanating from the small window. The icons and iconostasis at the altar front were still nailed to the floor, just as before. She crossed herself several times, bowed low to the floor, and opened the large central altar doors of the iconostasis.

She held back her breath. The golden communion

chalice was gone. So were the gold candlesticks and the big gold and silver crucifix. Fortunately, the tabernacle remained as before, in its place on the dusty white linen altar cloth. Above it the red lamp hung from the round ceiling by its thick golden chains.

There were withered flowers in the vases, probably the same ones from the very last time she and the other villagers attended Mass that terrible Palm Sunday. The bouquets of white daisies had turned a putrid brown, the leaves were transparent, and the pussy willows had long ago let go of their fuzzy balls, which were scattered all over the floor. She went outside to throw away the abandoned flowers and left the vases on the steps to air out.

Marusia stepped to the right of the altar, where a well-varnished door opened into the priest's sacristy. There he had kept his vestments and the ritual objects needed to celebrate the Mass. What had happened to Father Andrei? Did he die that horrible night, or was he alive in a refugee camp, or slowly losing his life in a filthy hospital? Did his crazy old mother, old Paraskevia, ever see him again?

Marusia opened the door to the closet and was glad that the vestments had not been touched. She knew where things were kept because she and the other *babysi* in the village had taken turns cleaning the church and mending the vestments. She fingered the rich gold brocade, then searched for a box she knew was hidden in a drawer and found that nobody had taken the other chalices and incense.

Really, it would have been such a low sin to steal the vestments and chalices and sell them for Western cigarettes, she thought. Only a rotten thief would sell his mother for those sinful, stinking cigarettes.

She lit a candle and left the room through another door that led into a cold, clammy area of the building that stank of peat moss and rancid water. From there, she climbed to the bell tower. The winding wrought iron staircase creaked and swung out each time she laid her heavy foot on a slippery stair. She was perspiring, but out of respect she kept her head covered with her cotton babushka.

In the tower the air was cooler, and from where she stood she could see the entire dilapidated village. It looked gray and seemed muzzled beneath the gauzy skies. Over to the east, the silent overgrown *kolhosp* hayfields were burnt blond, and rotting carcasses of straw bales were still visible. She shuddered when she realized that the red lights on the horizon were not planets or stars, but the twinkling red lights from the towers of Chornobyl.

Her eyes lingered on the tattered roofs of the motley homes, threatened now by the bent trees that folded over the buildings like brown ghosts with broken spines.

"I am in hell," Marusia said aloud. Her knees buckled, but she held her balance. "Lord, take me now." She beat her chest with her fist. "Take me so that I won't be alone anymore."

Marusia cried a little longer, then asked for forgiveness. She searched for her own house and saw the thin stream of smoke blowing hopefully out her chimney and up to the filthy sky where only God could see it. Maybe it will tickle the soles of an angel who will tug at the Lord's robe and point to where I am, she thought.

"Or maybe they'll hear me. Please God, let someone down there, hear me!" she called out. She grabbed two tufts of cotton she had brought from the house and plugged up her ears as best she could before trying to pull on the long rope. With the big fingers of both of her hands wrapped around the rope, she tugged at the ringer until the bells finally groaned and then swung into life and shocked the stillness of the air with their clanging.

Marusia's head vibrated and ached with the timbre. She rang and felt the rope cutting deep into her hands. Her chest hurt, and dizziness filled her head. When her ears buzzed with pain, she stopped. But she kept her vow and returned later that evening. She made it part of her personal vigil to ring the bells twice a day: once in the early morning, and again before the terrifying night fell.

In fact, Marusia looked forward to ringing the bells. She felt a great release in their melodic noise, and sometimes, because she knew she couldn't be heard over the sounds, she cried out loud to God and to the world and asked why she was forsaken in such misery. Often she was on the brink of cursing at God, but as each ring strengthened her bitterness, she cried and cried until she no longer felt so deeply the ache in her arms and in her heart. When the bells muted and no longer swayed, she wiped her tears, descended the stairway, and prayed before the iconostasis that the saints and the Virgin would forgive her hostility and that her anger at God would not scar her heart.

Two saints in particular were the objects of her concentrated prayers. In the evenings, she prayed to St. George, the dragon slayer, to protect her from the animals she heard on her walks home—shrill wolflike howls and mad bird screeches. And in the daytime she prayed to St. Nicholas, the Miracle Worker, to release her from her loneliness. "Or at least, remember me when I die," she whispered. A strange thought filtered into her prayers: She dared to think that when she died, no one would be there on the other side for her either, not even Jesus. "Forgive my sinful mind," she begged each time the thought intruded upon her devotions.

Chapter 13

DESPITE THE WARM WEATHER, Marusia kept her stove going. She had to believe that someone would turn up and see that a live human presence was in the village again.

Exactly four weeks after her arrival, she heard a knock on her door.

"Hey! Somebody in there?" a man's voice shouted. Marusia peeped out the window. He was a short, thin man dressed in blue fatigues and a white paper face mask. He slung a rifle over his left shoulder and pounded harder on the door. "Hello! Anyone there?"

Marusia was overjoyed. She opened the door. "*Slava Isusu Chrystu.* Yes, yes, somebody's here. Come in, come in."

"No, thanks. I saw the chimney smoke and I had come to see who's here."

She peered at him up close to see if she knew him,

and could see a thick black bush of a mustache above his face mask. "Are you from here? I don't seem to know you. . . ."

"No. I'm from Prypiat'. I was sent here to chase away the dogs with this. . . ." He patted the butt end of his rifle. "So, seen any dogs around?"

"No, I don't think so. Sometimes I hear sounds at night. Maybe those are the dogs howling. I'm not sure."

"How long have you been here."

"Almost a month."

"But why are you here? Do you have a permit from the council? Do you work for the plant?"

"No. I live here."

He laughed, lit a cigarette, and puffed it through his thin face mask, which was already dotted with brown nicotine spots. "Excuse me, *babo,* but this is a contaminated zone. No one is supposed to be here."

"Yes, but people work at the plant. And the government said we can return. . . ."

"Wait a minute! Just when did the government say that?"

"It's in the papers. I read it myself in Kyiv. The radiation wasn't so bad after all. Things are back to normal, so why shouldn't I come back to my house?" She wished she could talk to the man the way Zosia used to, firm and confident.

He shook his head. "Nobody said it was all right for you to come back. The real truth is, if you want to know, that things are so bad that all of us are doomed.

It's the end of the world, *babo.* Still, you're right—people work at the plant and live around there like before. But it stinks with radiation. Anyone else here?"

"No. Just me. I'm alone. Listen, my cow is gone. I'm sure she's dead. I need a new cow. And my pension. I haven't seen my money since I left here so long ago. . . ."

He coughed up some phlegm and pulled down his mask so he could spit into her bushes. "You're not officially supposed to be here."

"But I am now!"

"I don't know what to do for you. I'm just supposed to shoot dogs. Any dogs here?"

"No. None here. I used to have a dog, and a cow, and my cat, Myrrko. I used to have a son and grandchildren and even some chickens. I lost everything because of your damned radiation. So, now I'm telling you, I need my money and for you to do something and get me a new cow."

"Look *babo,* this isn't right. You have to leave. Watch this." He took out a small box that looked like a transistor radio and placed it above her head. "See this thing. It measures the radiation. Hear that crackling—sounds like an old man's snore? Radiation! I took it off a dead man after the explosion. Around here this little gauge is worth a fortune. Those bastards at the plant probably only have three in the whole stupid country, that's how crazy this explosion situation is. I'm going to sell this thing and get the hell out of this place. But listen." He positioned the instrument against the doorjamb. "Sh. Here that? See how high the numbers go? That's the poison. That's radiation, dear heart. You got it, I got it."

She was getting impatient. "I don't care about your toy. I'm here on my own land where I'll die. Make yourself useful and tell your chiefs that I'm here and I'll starve soon and I want a cow. My son died because of that explosion. They can compensate me with a cow."

He shook his head. "Well, I just don't know," he said patiently, then sniffed the soup that was simmering on her woodstove. "Hey, you can't cook here. It's poison. You'll die of madness and they'll come here and arrest you and shoot you like I do the dogs." He searched his pocket for a cigarette. "You know the joke, 'How do you make chicken Kyiv? You hold the chicken out the window for a few minutes.' Hah!" He laughed so hard he started to cough.

She crossed her arms. "Yes, funny. Then why didn't they tell us how bad it was?"

He shook his head. "I have to go. All I can do is tell the deputy at the plant that you're here. That's all. Take care."

"Thank you, sir." She tried to grab his hand, but he stepped back from her grasp as though she had the plague. "Have something to eat, at least."

"No, thanks. You take care of yourself." He hurried away from her house. "Stubborn old bitch," she heard him mutter.

After he left, she heard the popping sounds of gunshots. She wondered if that's how the animals on her land had been killed, or had they died from the poison in the air.

But at least someone knows I'm here, she thought, and she realized how very quiet it was once again.

HE RETURNED ONCE more about three weeks later. Marusia heard the short crackles from his rifle early in the morning. She stood at her window and saw a pack of dogs running past her front yard. One lagged behind, a thin, white German shepherd who sniffed and lingered at her gate for only a minute before she saw its skeletal body shudder and hit the ground. The dog's upturned face stared straight at her, and she heard it whimper. It didn't whine or yelp, but uttered a more dignified moan from its slender, pulsating throat. A truck pulled up alongside the animal. The dogcatcher leaned out of the passenger side and shot it square in the head.

"Got him!" He jumped out of his truck, then lifted the limp hind legs with his gloved hands and threw its body in the back of the pickup. Marusia opened her door and held her nose. She couldn't help staring at the heap of dog and cat bodies piled on top of some rabbits and an animal she thought was a small pig.

"See a cow back there?" he laughed. "Take it if you see one."

She stood back from the stench.

"Hey! I told them about you. But that's all I can do.

Listen, want a ride to Prypiat'? You can get the train back to Kyiv."

"No, thank you," she said, and turned away from him again.

"Those roving dogs are wild. You could be eaten alive."

She turned and waved from her front steps. "Not with you around to protect me."

He laughed. "See you. Or maybe not in this place anymore! Maybe in hell, sooner than here! Okh, hell can't be so bad after this place, that's for sure." He waved at her, beeped his horn, and left.

She was sad to see him go. After the dust settled on the dirt road, and the thick silence closed in on her once again, she wondered if she shouldn't have gone with him.

Chapter 14

MARUSIA'S EYES ACHED constantly and itched. The irritation wearied her so much that one evening she had to slice two pieces of a potato she was about to boil for her dinner and apply them to her swollen eyelids. The poultice eased her pain somewhat. She found release in a heavy dark sleep void of urgent dreams and did not awake until dusk.

"Okh," Marusia said, disoriented and surprised to find the potato slices over her eyes. "I have to ring the bells." She grabbed a candle and a match and hurried to the church. On the way, she heard crickets in the grass and saw the faint white half-moon in the sky.

She climbed the stairs. High in the tower it seemed darker than usual. She lit the candle and waited for the wax to drip on the counter where she would plant the light. She heard a low humming sound and stumbled back on something that felt like a rope. She heard another screech, and the rope came alive and whipped itself out of her path.

Then she heard a dull thump followed by a low cry that sounded like an old woman's moan.

"What's that?" she yelled.

She peered into the growing darkness. Two coal-lit eyes stared at her from atop a ceiling beam.

"Oh, hello *kotyku,*" she said. She brought her dripping candle closer to its face. The cat's fur stuck up in spikes as though it had tried to wash the poison out of its coat. It sat there watching her, slowly heaving its caved-in chest.

"How long have you been here, *kotyku?* Are you crazy, too? Like the dogs. And me," she said. "Well, be careful that the man with the gun doesn't get you."

The cat meowed, but softer than before.

She was afraid to touch it. It hissed its fear, then scampered away down the stairs and out her sight.

The next morning, she brought along a small bowl of powdered milk mixed with water and left it at the foot of the winding stairs. The cat jumped down from its place in the shadows and briefly rubbed against her ankles like an electric shock before it darted straight for the dish. It sniffed the milk for a long while before lapping it up.

"Oh, once you were a pretty one," Marusia said. The cat was matted and filthy. Its front paws were caked with dried blood, and both of its ears were torn. "You've been fighting," she told it. "Be careful—there are wild animals out there. Fierce, like bears." The cat looked up at her, blinked its filmy eyes, and purred.

"You're welcome. Now, excuse me, I have to ring the bells," she said, climbing the stairs. She rang them for a long time and was surprised to find the cat waiting for her when she came down from the tower. "Well, how nice. But are you deaf? I swear I will be in no time." Her body swayed from dizziness, and she had to steady herself against the clammy wall.

The cat followed her inside the church but stopped short of going outside the door. "No? Stay here, then. You're such a skinny one. I wish I could feed you so that you could plump up like a pillow." She herself ate only once a day—mostly from her stored supply of dry staples and what was left of the canned vegetables she had preserved in the summers before the accident.

She thought about her limited pantry. She did have jars of applesauce, green beans, peas and carrots left, and a few more jars of compotes she had made of dried apples, pears and apricots. But those supplies would get very low in a matter of weeks. She feared the approaching winter. "Getting cold out there." She hesitated in the doorway.

"Well, then, I'll just go back to Chornobyl and demand that they give me some food. Or maybe that *zaraza* dogcatcher will be back. But it's been three weeks already. . . . would he let an old woman starve?"

"Yes, he would!" She turned toward the cat, who meowed its sickly croak at her. "I won't starve. And you are invited to share my food. I won't starve! I haven't lived this long to die like that. Don't you worry! Sleep well." She stood in front of the iconostasis again, bowed low, and left for home.

From then on, Marusia brought the cat milk every morning. Sometimes the animal came to her, other times she had to search for it when she found the milk untouched. She was surprised how much she missed it when she didn't see its mangy body curved over the bowl at least once a day.

HER MORNINGS WERE spent gardening. Her hoe sometimes turned up old potatoes, green and withered, that she took in gladly. She would wash and boil them carefully. Everything counted.

She liked to hoe in the early morning after she had rung the bells, before the sun beamed its heavy rays on her. She searched and found some old seeds in her kitchen for beets and squash which would survive the light frosts. She sprinkled holy water over the dirt, so that the seeds would gain strength and not be poisoned by the evil lurking in the soil.

ONE MORNING SHE didn't see the cat in the church, but found it staring at her in her garden. It looked grayer than in the dark tower, and its fur was slicked back with wet streaks, as though it had groomed itself before coming to visit her. Then it moved, pulling at the neck of a large dead rabbit.

The cat dropped its gift at Marusia's feet.

"What's this? Do you want me bury that thing or eat it?" She laughed and prodded it with her hoe. It looked healthy enough, but who could know.

"I'll make it for you," she said. "You'll be my guest. My first one since I came back home."

She found that the rabbit's skin tore off easily enough, and its flesh was pink. She roasted the legs and boiled a generous portion of potatoes and carrots.

She didn't notice the cat silently following her into the house. It sat on the sink, where Katia's cat used to rest, and it stared at the old woman, ready to pounce.

"We're going to die, so let's at least eat well and look good in our coffins." She smiled at the cat. "But who will bury me? Will you?" She laughed and felt giddy because of the live presence of the animal. "Will you drag me into a field and bury me? No, I suppose not. Dogs are better at burying. Cats—what good are they? Except that you at least let me talk to you. Oh, and you did catch this feast for me." She thought briefly about the dogcatcher and hoped that she wouldn't be forced to turn the cat in to him.

For dinner they shared the rabbit. Marusia declared that it tasted as sweet and fine as the ones her father caught for Christmas dinner. "Not one difference," she told the cat, who scuttled to a window ledge and licked its bloody paws.

Chapter 15

THE END OF summer was hot and fetid. Marusia believed that her life was saved because of the garden. Whenever she felt the unbearable loneliness weigh her down and the sinking feeling of betrayal, she worked in her little patch of land, and its capacity for life humbled her. Once her hoe cut deep into a long blond horse-radish root she had planted years before the horrible event. It would be precious for Easter breakfast, and she dug it out, amazed that it was over two feet in length. Another time she found a neglected patch of tiny wild strawberries but decided not to eat them. It was enough for her merely to look at them in quiet reverence.

She cried more in her garden than inside her house. Whenever she poked seeds into the overturned earth or patted a mound of dirt down around potato eyes she thought of her son, and always cursed her luck that she could not bury him here at home.

September was nearly over, and the air was still warm and balmy. The first turnip appeared in its row next to a large green squash that had come up between the snarly new potatoes. Marusia was harvesting some of them and threw them into her battered wheelbarrow. She thanked God on her knees for the harvest and buried her hands into the silt, where she felt one ribbony earthworm caressing her fingers.

Her beets were meager—small pinkish beetroots only the size of baby fists. She dug them up anyway. The tomatoes were small and a sickly greenish-yellow. The onions had all died early in the season. Still, she hoped that more potatoes and cabbages would come through all right before the first frost.

In the past, autumn had been a bountiful time for collecting the white mushrooms that had made Starylis famous. Marusia spotted them growing wild along the forest paths she sometimes took on her way to and from the church. Unlike the living things in her garden, they looked large and healthy with their rich and feathery umbrella caps. She feared them, as though the mushrooms thriving in the unholy and evil soil were a defiant rebuke.

When she wasn't working, Marusia felt ill. Her joints were achy like a flu that wouldn't leave her body. She coughed too much, and her eyes itched and felt dry despite the tears she shed whenever she prayed for Yurko and her lost, scattered family and neighbors.

There were many harsh moments when her prayers

and tears were not enough balm to soothe the loneliness that overwhelmed her. Sometimes she would chew on the hemp gum or, better, locate the last of the fine, mellow rose-petal vodka she had kept hidden all these years. It was Yurko's last batch. The recipe was handed down to her and her son from her husband, and every time she allowed herself a forbidden sip, she always thought of the man she had had the misfortune to marry—his strong good looks, his white teeth and easy laughter that rang out every time he coaxed her to drink another glass of the evil brew. In their early years together, they would dance after drinking a bottle, and he would kiss her shy lips and hold her firm young body close enough so that she could hear his sweet words caressing her ears with the scent of rose petals.

The fragrant elixir laced her tongue, and she knew that if he appeared in front of her right now, she would still offer him the world. "I'm such a fool for that bad man," she cried. "And he would leave me again for that *kurva!*" She downed the rest of her glass, and the warmth of the liquor soothed her chest. "This is all you left me, you bastard. A son who is now a ghost like you, and this damn vodka." She cried a bit more, then felt tired enough to fall into a deep sleep for which she was grateful the next day.

THE CAT BECAME her companion and visited her more often at home than in the church. It kept its distance from her and still would not let her pet it, nor would it rub itself again against the old woman's ankles. But at unexpected times it came close enough for her to hear its bronchial purr. Marusia saw that its eyes flowed with mucus and heard its consumptive breath rattling heavily. One time the cat breathed and whistled through its nose so loudly that Marusia, feeling sorry for its misery, gave it a bowl of warm potato soup broth and boiled a spoonful of the precious rice she kept hidden in the back of the cupboard.

The cat slept well after eating the soup, but its nose still dripped. Often it limped and kept its tail, clotted with burrs, upright in the air to help its balance. Its head was usually bloodied with fresh sores. Marusia caught it constantly licking its paws and hind legs and noticed that more clumps of fur were missing on its shivering body.

The breezes were turning cooler. It was time to get ready for the long, lonely winter. She would have to bring in more firewood from the shed because she had used so much keeping the chimney smoking. The kindling box was low, and that meant chopping some firewood into smaller pieces. Then she had to seal up her windows and doorways with cloth strips. The very thought of these preparations tired her. Maybe, she thought, I could just take some wood from the neighbor's shed. But no, she cautioned herself. They will be back, and then what will they say to me? They'll call me a thief, and I'll get angry, and that would be a fine welcome for them. No—I'll get by even with the stove going in the daytime. Someone might come back and see that I'm here. She could not believe that no one would come.

SEPTEMBER MELTED INTO October, and the mild autumn sharpened into brisker weather. One noontime, Marusia had just returned from ringing the church bells and was in her house boiling some cabbage for her soup when she heard the cowbells jingle. The sound startled her, and at first she dismissed it, thinking it was only the wind shaking the bells. Then she heard an impatient knock followed by a woman's demanding voice calling, "Is there anybody alive in this house?"

Marusia dropped her wooden mixing spoon and hurried to the door. On her doorstep stood a much older Evdokia Zenoviivna, carrying a cardboard suitcase without handles that was held closed with a thick rope. Behind her was old man Oleh. He looked the same, but Marusia was a bit shocked to see that Evdokia had aged and wasn't as stout as when she last saw her at her granddaughter's wedding right before the catastrophe.

"You came back!" Marusia shouted, grabbing the suitcase to set it down. She and her old friends hugged together. "Welcome back! Welcome back home!"

"*Slava Isusu Christu,*" said the old man, his face ruddy. He rubbed his chapped hands and sniffed the air. "Cooking something?"

"Yes, come in! Sit down, sit down. I'm so happy to

see you!" Marusia's eyes blurred with tears. "Oh Lord, how I prayed for someone besides me to come back here."

Evdokia and her husband sat down near the wood-stove and took off their boots. Marusia rushed to fetch them some felt *kaptsi* for their feet.

"Well, we would've come earlier, but my old man here had to take so many leak stops."

Marusia was relieved to see Evdokia's high cheeks bloom and redden and that familiar pug nose twitch when her old friend lifted the soup lid and sniffed the pot. "Smells good, but needs more salt, Marusia," Evdokia said. She sat down at the table. "But thank God we came before it got too dark. We heard the church bells when we came to the village and I felt so much better. I said to my old man, 'See, we're not all dead yet.' Then we saw your chimney smoking. No one else's, although we knocked on just about everybody's door along the way."

Marusia kept crying and wrung her hands and rocked back and forth with joy. "I'm all alone here, I came back first. Just me. Nobody else. Now you're here. *Slava Bohu.* Praise God!"

"But how did you manage by yourself like this?" Evdokia asked.

"I don't know. I'm so alone. I prayed someone would return. But, even better, I'm so glad it's you, my friends!"

Marusia insisted that the old couple sit at the table, where she set out three shot glasses and a special bottle of the rose-petal vodka she and Yurko had prepared so many years ago. She served them huge portions of the cabbage soup that was bubbling in her pot.

The three of them raised their glasses. "Bless you. You came back. *Dai Bozhe,*" Marusia said. They downed their drinks.

"Okh, that was good," Evdokia said. "It's been so long since I had that."

Marusia refilled the glasses.

"Let's see," Evdokia continued, "the last time we saw you was in town, before we left on those bumpy buses. Yoy, my butt still hurts from that ride!" She and her husband slurped the hot soup. Evdokia took out a hard piece of dark bread from the pocket of her sweater and gave half of it to her husband. She dunked the other half into her bowl. "We ended up in the Carpathians," she said.

"Karpaty!" repeated the man dreamily. His mustache was wet and dripping from the soup he drank without using the spoon Marusia had given him.

"The mountains! Is that where our people went? I was in Kyiv."

"That would've been better. Many of us were put in with families near the Polish border. They spoke so differently from us, who could understand anything? But so many of us won't be back. Old Paraskevia, the priest's mother, got sick. She refused to eat anything. They took her to some hospital. I heard she didn't last long after that."

Marusia made the sign of the cross.

Evdokia named many others from Starylis who had died—too many young ones who caught leukemia. "Well, my son-in-law gone as well," Evdokia said, her eyes streaming. "He had cancer anyway. He was a commie, but you know toward the end, he asked for a priest.

"And you know, Marusia, Hanna stayed with us for a while. But that wasn't good enough for her. She went to Lviv—the big city. She lost the baby, and then her stupid husband got sent back to clean up in Chornobyl. We never heard again from him. She got involved with some Party big shot—an old fart who left his wife and six children. She's living with him in a *dacha* in Odesa. And before I left, her mother—my own daughter— was about to move down there with them. What sins! Of course, we didn't want to go with them."

Oleh laughed.

"This old fool is too stupid to know anything. Just as well," said Evdokia, grinning at her husband.

"My Yurko is dead," Marusia said. She sobbed through her own story, and appreciated her friends' echoes of sympathy.

After a while the tears were wiped, and Oleh asked for more soup and poured himself another shot glass full of vodka.

"How is my home? Is it all right? Tell me if it's not," Evdokia said.

"I don't really know. I never went into anyone's house except my own and the church."

"I worried about my house. I had my vegetables and my root cellar. It may have all gone bad. And this one here"—she pointed to Oleh—"cried himself to sleep over his wine and his still. But my cow is dead I suppose," she said quietly. "And my pigs and ducks . . ."

"My bees!" Oleh cried out.

"I'm sorry, I don't know. I just couldn't go into the houses to look. I went into the Metrenkos' when I first came back—for only a few minutes—and it made me so sad and lonely that I didn't have the heart . . . you know. I was so lonely."

Evdokia nodded her head. "Well, we should go back to our own home. I don't care how bad it is. I won't sleep until I know that it's at least standing." She rose and collected the soup bowls.

"Leave that, I'll take care of it. Stay here tonight. You can see your house in the morning."

"No. I want to see it now. Hey you, old man," she scolded her husband, "leave that bottle alone and put on your boots."

"Wait." Marusia jumped out of her chair. "Let me get a candle. I'll go with you."

The three of them walked down the road in the cool darkness. Evdokia lived three houses away from Marusia, and just like her, she fell on her knees and kissed the earth before entering through the door. Oleh laughed and shuffled a little dance, his mouth black except for one front tooth. Inside, Evdokia lit the candles that were left over from the last Easter, because there was no electricity. She stumbled around until she found a kerosene lamp and set it on her kitchen table. The house was musty. Evdokia immediately attacked a large cobweb with a broom. A dried dead spider fell to the ground, and its brittle shell shattered when it hit the floor.

"What a mess! *Feh!*" Evdokia complained. Although the light was dim, her quick eyes darted around to see if anything was stolen. She hurried to the pantry. "Well, looks all right. But who knows. . . ." she muttered. "My food!" she said. She lit another kerosene lamp and coaxed Marusia to follow her down to the root cellar. But something made Marusia stay in the room with the old man. She watched Oleh head toward his favorite rocker, which was where he left it, in front of the brown-tiled stove. It was dark in that corner, and he didn't bother to light a candle and set it near him. He sat down, found his pipe in his coat pocket, but didn't know where he had left his matches.

He sat there sucking on the cold pipe, a hungry child on his mother's nipple. Marusia could hear the contentment of his smackings and see how his cheeks sank in a bit to draw out the last taste of the old tobacco when he sucked harder. She watched as he looked around his old home, felt its safety, and heaved one more sigh—a large one. When his wife returned to ask him if he wanted the stove lit, he wouldn't move for her.

EVDOKIA STAYED THE night in Marusia's house. They left the old man sitting in his chair. In the morning, they returned to where he waited. They decided not to practice the custom of washing the dead because water was too scarce, so they bundled him in a blanket and carried him in Marusia's wheelbarrow to the cemetery behind the church. He was light enough, so it was easy to lower him into a shallow pit they dug in Evdokia's family plot. Marusia made a cross out of three small branches tied with some chicken wire she found. They lit candles and sang the *Vichnaia Pamiat'* for his soul before burying him.

"I wish we had some flowers," Evdokia said. "We'll plant some in the spring, and I'll bring him a fresh bouquet. You'll just have to wait, old man," she said to the fresh mound of earth.

That evening at Marusia's kitchen table, Evdokia shared a bottle of mead that Oleh had kept hidden under their bed. "I think it was that damn walk that did it to him. He was too old," Evdokia said. "You'd think that he might have had a few more minutes with me to say good-bye. He should've called me, damn him."

Evdokia poured another round. "He was always in a hurry to get somewhere." She stared at the bottle still half full of the thick, syrupy alcohol. "That Oleh knew how to make a great wine, and he always held his bottles with more gentleness than he ever held me.

"And you know what else? He always loved his smokes more than me, too. It's true, I never knew how to kiss that man as good as that old pipe of his." She took his pipe from her pocket and kissed its base. "Now it's mine. My rival. It's the last thing he touched."

Evdokia was silent for a moment, and so was Marusia. "I want to be buried with this," she said, and began to cry.

Marusia stared at her glass and listened to her friend's sadness throughout the bitter and cold night.

Chapter 16

EVDOKIA'S GRIEF KEPT her at Marusia's house. She slept in Yurko and Zosia's room and complained of chills at night because the stove was barely warm. "So, she hasn't changed at all since I last saw her," Marusia grumbled to herself. "Just the same—always saying what she thinks without thinking first."

When she felt stronger, Evdokia went back to her house. Marusia went along with her, and together they closely assessed her pantry, root cellar and beehives. The yard was covered with tiny hillocks of dead bees, but the rich honey was ready to collect. It was decided that the two women would pool their food reserves, sharing their canned goods and preserves for the winter, or until they were able to contact an official who would send them supplies.

Evdokia was generous—she had an untouched pantry filled with cans of caviar from the Black Sea and sardines and herring from Israel, and a large tin of squid that she had never tried before in her life. "From Italy," she boasted. Whenever her son-in-law traveled on official Soviet business, he always brought back exotic foodstuffs as a way to appease Evdokia, since she used to openly blame him for turning her daughter into a Bolshevik. They decided they would save the seafood for Christmas eve dinner and also drink a bottle of Evdokia's *sovietskoye champanskoye* if the two of them made it to Christmas on January seventh.

Marusia believed that Evdokia had enough dry wood for one winter. "It might be wiser to stay together in one house and conserve the wood," Marusia suggested. "At least this first winter together."

Evdokia frowned. "I want to stay in my own house, even though I'm still afraid my dead husband might visit me in the night and bother me to bring him something to eat the way he used to, the fool."

"But your house is so much bigger than mine and takes more heat."

"So, I'll close off some of my rooms," Evdokia countered. Marusia knew why she did not want to live with her. It would be too cramped, and she had too small a kitchen. They would kill each other in such a closet of a kitchen! And she knew that most of all, Evdokia hated the cat who hung around Marusia's garden and sat on a window ledge, where it watched them through the window.

"That cat is a devil," she had said to Marusia. "It scares me." Marusia didn't want to shoo it away too often—she liked its presence, sometimes in preference to Evdokia's blabbering ways. But the cat would at times sense that it wasn't wanted and would hide from them for a few days until it forgave the old women's rudeness and returned.

"I would feel better if you stayed with me," Marusia said. She surveyed the uncut logs in Evdokia's shed and dreaded having to help her slice the gnarly wood with Oleh's rusty bow saw. "Stay through the worst of the season, then go back to your home in March or so."

Evdokia reluctantly agreed, although Marusia could tell she believed it wouldn't work. Her fears were proven true from the beginning. The women quarreled and insisted on their own ways, which they acted out almost deliberately at the inconvenience of the other. For Evdokia, Marusia's house was "too damn cold." She was used to blazing fires heating her house until she had to open a window to cool it down.

Marusia didn't approve of the way her friend wasted water for cooking—you didn't really have to rinse the dishes so much, she often grumbled in an undertone that always caught Evdokia's ear. Worse was Evdokia's constant chattering, a bona fide *nunya,* a blabbermouth, Marusia thought, who has to give her unwanted advice and opinions on every single little detail in the universe. And here she goes complaining about everyone . . . even Father Andrei who could be dead! *Nunya!* She wanted to shout out. *Nunya,* grab your tongue and tear it out!

Still, they shared their meals, preserved the last of the honey from Oleh's dead bees, and took turns ringing the bells. Evdokia felt safer ringing in the mornings; she didn't like to go near the church in the evenings so near to where her husband was buried. "He might come and scare me to death for a joke," Evdokia said in earnest. "He'd do something like that, you know."

"But the cemetery is holy earth," Marusia said. She also didn't care to ring the bells in the bleak evenings, now that the weather was cooler and the sun disappeared sooner into the swiftly darkening skies.

"Ah, but we never gave him a real funeral." Evdokia's eyes flashed with triumph. "So, his soul is still wandering. Anyway, even so, it takes forty days for the soul to go to heaven."

Marusia had nothing to say to that and agreed to take the evening shift.

THE WOMEN MANAGED well enough despite their physical ailments. Evdokia experienced sore eyes and scratchy skin, and Marusia still coughed up phlegm, and her head throbbed from the cold. When the miseries of their bodies subsided, they were plagued by loneliness. Evdokia cried in the middle of sentences that had nothing to do with death, and Marusia would, in her turn, feel so lost she had to retreat to her own room and chew on the hemp gum to quiet her nerves.

The full moon in November brought a hard frost, and the women spent less time outdoors. Marusia still hoped that the dogcatcher would show up again, or some other people from the village or officials from Chornobyl. "Oh, to have fresh milk again," she complained too often to Evdokia. She longed for her grandchildren. She missed their hugs and wet kisses laced with candy. She still hadn't unpacked the suitcase she'd brought back with her. She couldn't bear to find Tarasyk's hair or the big white ribbon Katia used to wear. Loneliness ate at her soul, and Evdokia's taciturn whines and howls of grief tested Marusia's belief in deliverance. She secretly wished that the cat would come jump on her lap or caress her cheek once in a while.

After the frost, the next few days were brighter and warmer, and a genuine thaw came with the new moon. Marusia felt a surge of cleanliness in the air after she returned from ringing the evening bells. She looked up at the diamond-lustered stars in the sky and almost felt hopeful again.

Evdokia had dinner ready—potatoes fried in sunflower oil with a cinnamon-like fragrance to it. "This is wonderful," said Marusia. She felt her spirits restored. "What did you do?"

Evdokia eagerly watched Marusia eat. "So, you like it." She smiled broadly. "Well, I put in some spices. Much better, eh?"

"Oh, did you go back to your house and find some?"

"Not exactly. I went further down the road to my neighbor's. You remember Fedya the co-op owner? His wife had the most beautiful kitchen. She was a wonderful cook. And you know why—well, because she had all of these spices. Things I never heard of like *kuew-ree.* She has red and yellow *kuew-ree.*"

"How in the world do you know?"

"Oh, we often used to go to their home for *praznyky,* the holiday parties. And what a fancy cook. After the war, for a time, she worked in a hotel restaurant in the Crimea—that's where she met Fedya when he was on vacation. What a cook she was! She met Frenchmen who visited the hotel and they gave her recipes."

Marusia had heard various rumors about Fedya's wife, but she didn't say anything. "So where did you get the spices?" She put down her spoon. "You went in and took them!"

"Look, what good does it do to leave these things to rot? Marusia, I was thinking. Maybe you and I are here, but it may be that nobody else will return. Maybe everyone died off, all our generation—gone! None of the young ones will come back here. Why would they?"

Marusia pursed her lips and winced at hearing her own forbidden thoughts spoken aloud in Evdokia's grating tone, shouted full into her face. She pushed the plate of potatoes away from her and crossed her arms.

"Look," Marusia said, "You came. I came. Others will come. Wait until spring. It's too hard to travel now.

Then what will happen? We live off everyone's food and they come back and send us to Siberia as thieves. No! A sin. No!"

"But this is an emergency! You've heard of people starving in the snow, and yet it is an unwritten law of God that people in need can take from others in an emergency. Like the hunters lost in the woods who happen to find an abandoned house. They eat the food, use the wood for heat, live, write a thank-you note, and that's it. Off they go. Be well."

Marusia glared at her friend. "Cinnamon or *kuer-ski* or whatever you put in the potatoes is not going to save my life. A plain potato, even a cold one, is just fine by me."

"Oh, all right," Evdokia said. "But we do need powdered milk. We're running low. We need medicines. You still have that grippe, and my eyes itch so much I want to shoot someone. And what are we going to do for water? Maybe what's in that pump is poisoned. Maybe we should search for mineral water in bottles."

Marusia stood up and stoked the coals in the stove in silence.

"Oh, be practical, Marusia! If I hadn't come along, you would have had to do this soon enough. Any day now we may be on our deathbeds. It's not a sin to take what we need to survive!"

Evdokia was right—Marusia had to yield on this. The water was bad—tinged with rust and certainly worse. Even boiling it didn't help it much. Evdokia persuaded Marusia that they could at least visit some of the houses tomorrow and "see what's around in case of an emergency." Marusia was silent. "That's all I'm saying. So we know where to go in case we need something," Evdokia urged.

"And Marusia," Evdokia said after she won. "You had to admit—those were good potatoes!"

THE NEXT DAY Evdokia eagerly led the way inside Fedya's house. Marusia had been in it a few times before, but only because other villagers were collectively invited for a baptism or an anniversary feast. The kitchen was large and sunny, and the cupboards were filled with spice bottles with rubber stoppers, the sort found in a scientist's laboratory. "Look." Evdokia jubilantly held up a ring of dried mushrooms that were hung on a string. "There's more." She held up canned herring and powdered milk. "And the best prize of all—water from Vichy. See, I told you there'd be water!"

"Well, maybe we'll take the water for emergencies," Marusia said.

"And the mushrooms."

"No, that's not needed." But Evdokia already wore the string around her neck.

"This is only the beginning," said Evdokia. "They had so much! They were like rich Americans! Come here." She grabbed Marusia's hand and dragged her into a bedroom where an entire wall was covered with clothing that hung from a long iron bar suspended from chains drilled into the high ceiling. The clothes were protected with a thick sheet of clear plastic which Evdokia lifted up. She eagerly grabbed the skirt of a pink chiffon ballgown. "Look at this wealth!" She took out a coat and blew on its collar. "Mink!"

"Did she get those things from the French chefs too?" Marusia said dryly.

Evdokia giggled like a naughty girl. "Oh, look at this." She took out a low-cut red velvet evening gown with wide sleeves trimmed in black fur and a train. "Oh wouldn't I look beautiful in this one?" She held it up to herself and admired her reflection in the mirror of a large vanity table that was crowded with exotic perfumes and vibrantly colored lipsticks. Evdokia smiled and showed her yellow cracked teeth beneath her puffy red eyes. "Well, once I was pretty. Now *starist' ne radist'*, old age isn't happiness, as they say."

Marusia was uncomfortable. She thought it was like picking over the things left by a dead person. "I thought we were only going to search for necessary food."

Evdokia ignored her. "I used to be quite a dancer when I was young. Oh, well, there's no one to dance with here, anyway." She sadly put the dress back on its hanger.

"Not with me, that's for sure," Marusia said. She left the bedroom. "I'm going back home," she called out. She debated taking the mineral water with her but decided not to. "We know where it is in case we really do need it." She felt better about her decision. Marusia was out the door and halfway home before she turned around to hear Evdokia's *koo-koos* behind her.

"Wait for me! Hey! *Koo-koo!*" She came up to her friend, holding two bottles of Vichy water. "You forgot these." Marusia didn't say anything until she noticed Evdokia's shawl—a bright turquoise-and-white paisley-fringed one that was draped over her shabby brown woolen coat.

"I never saw that on you before."

"Oh, I think it suits my age better than that red dress."

Marusia faced Evdokia. "You can't take people's things! I don't care how our government allows it or how poor we are in this world . . . it's still a sin."

"We are not in the real world anymore!" Evdokia shouted back. "This is an emergency . . . just like it was during the war. Worse. At least there were armies to fight for us, but here it's only you and me. Two defense-less old women!"

"How is stealing that shawl going to help us?"

"I might have to barter it someday. Maybe your friend, the dogshooter, needs to be bribed. He might come back."

Marusia spat on the ground in anger. She started to walk home alone.

"It's an emergency because you keep your damn house so cold I could die from pneumonia. Not from the radiation either!" Evdokia screamed. "Because of you, I'll die!"

Marusia started to say that she should at least have the decency to steal something black for mourning, but forgot. Instead, her face beamed into a smile.

Evdokia caught up to her friend and stared at her. "What's the matter with you?" she asked, breathless, turning around to see.

Coming from the woods was a woman holding a sack over her shoulder like *D'id Moroz,* Grandfather Winter. She was dressed in black, her face and hair covered by a severe black knit scarf that wound around her head into a turban above her horizontal, knitted black brows.

"*Slava Isusu Chrystu,*" Slavka Lazorska said, putting her sack down on the snow-dusted ground. "I could hear you screaming all the way in the village, so I took the shortcut through the woods to see if I could help stop the fistfight or maybe mend some wounds."

The women embraced one another. "It's good to hear all that yelling," Lazorska teased. "I knew that I was definitely back in Starylis."

Marusia's smile was radiant. "Come to my house. I'll make a welcome dinner."

"Yes, and we'll share with you some wonderful vodka that even you didn't know about, Marusia," Evdokia put in.

Marusia laughed. "Well, I'm glad you're here now *Dokhtor.* Otherwise, Evdokia and I would have killed one another and you would have returned and be all alone."

She grabbed Lazorska's sack, and the three women linked arms on their walk to Marusia's.

Chapter 17

LAZORSKA WAS RELUCTANT to move in with the two. Having spent so long in cramped rooms, she said she yearned to be back in her own home, where she could stay up all night if she chose to, which Marusia well understood to mean not be bothered by the others' complaints and bickering.

She looked thinner, gaunt, and her braided hair had turned completely gray. Even the fine hairs above her lips had turned white, though her fierce eyebrows had remained as black as crow feathers. She didn't say much about her experiences after the evacuation, but whatever she survived had aged her threefold. She moved more slowly and kept her mouth shut in a grimace of pain.

She did say that she had been sent to Moscow for a while, where she grew weak from living in the city. From there she had gone on to live with some distant relatives in Kharkiv, and when she saw how hard their lives were, she found her way home as soon as she was able to gain her strength.

"And that is all," she sighed.

"Were you sick in Moscow?" Evdokia asked.

"Yes. To the bones," Lazorska said, then fell silent.

"Did you see my grandchildren with Zosia in Moscow, maybe?" Marusia asked.

Lazorska shook her head. "I hardly saw anyone from here. The few I knew died or were sent to other places. It was chaos where I was."

The women didn't ask anything else. They didn't want to pry into Lazorska's guarded, mysterious life.

Lazorska again declared that she would stay in her own house. "I have enough firewood. And I have loads of dried corn husks which make an excellent heat. I have enough wood for two, maybe three winters, and you're welcome to share."

"Thank you," Evdokia said. "Then I'll be moving back into my own place too." She looked directly at Marusia.

Marusia would not beg her to stay. She looked down at her hands in her lap and began a long monologue about her first days alone in the village, but Lazorska sat inert as though she hadn't a heard a word. "I have to rest now," she whispered.

"I'll go with you," Evdokia said. Marusia was surprised at how abandoned she felt when they left.

But on her evening walks to and from the bell ringing, Marusia was happy to see three chimneys smoking that mild winter. "Much better." She smiled. "Almost like a real neighborhood."

THE WOMEN DECIDED to celebrate their first Christmas Eve — January sixth — together at Evdokia's home. It was the custom to serve twelve meatless dishes in honor of the apostles, but because they were living off food that was dwindling, the women decided that each individual item on their plates would have to do instead of twelve separate lavish courses. "And we'll have to sing the carols to one another," Evdokia joked when the women sat down at her table. Lazorska seemed sullen throughout the meal, and hardly touched the food or the flat *sovietskoye champanskoye* Evdokia had kept from three Christmases ago.

After the prayers were recited and the *prosfora* — bread dipped in honey — was passed around, they ate in a tense, meditative silence. Marusia studied the slow dripping of the beeswax candle that was placed on top of the *kolach,* the Christmas bread, but decided against removing the candle.

Lazorska picked at the tiny bones of her small portion of tinned herring. She startled the quiet by dropping her fork on her plate. "Where's the extra place setting?" Her eyes were red and accusing.

Marusia and Evdokia stared stupidly at the frail angry woman in front of them.

"I'll get it," Evdokia stammered.

"No, stay where you are." Lazorska got up from her chair and frowned as though the pain she felt was an annoyance. She touched her chest then stood straight. "Where?" She headed for the cupboard. "In here?" She took out several dishes and bowls and tiny saucers and haphazardly placed them on the table and on the empty chairs. Then she stooped and lined them up in a row on the floor.

"*Dokhtor,* please don't bother," said Evdokia.

"These are for all the dead, everywhere." She carried the rest of the plates outside. Two brightly colored ceramic bowls rolled across the steps. A large wooden platter with hand-painted red poppies was hastily tossed and tumbled on top of a tree stump, and she pitched several small plates on the snowy ground.

"What's the matter with her?" Evdokia demanded. She followed Lazorska outside.

"Come back, you'll catch cold," Marusia shouted after her. The front yard looked eerie and still in the winter twilight, which closed around the skeletal figure of Lazorska in a moon trance, stomping around in the snow. When she finished she stood for a while in the yard, looking up at the sky and breathing in the crisp air, her hands on her narrow, bony hips. "Look," she said. "It's so cold, the stars are shivering." She laughed to herself, then calmly went back into the house, but stopped to mutter, "Or shivering like children from fear of the wolf. . . ."

"I'm very sorry, I should've remembered," Evdokia

appealed to Lazorska. "My head is everywhere these days except on my shoulders. . . ."

Lazorska sank into a chair near the big brown-tiled stove, where she took off her drenched *kaptsi* and tugged on her boots. "It doesn't matter anymore."

"No, no. What an idiot I am. I should have remembered. I mean, my husband died. I should've left a plate out for him." She turned to Marusia and shrugged.

"I forgot one for my son, too," Marusia whispered to herself. "I can't believe he's gone. I can't."

"I'll be going now," Lazorska said. Her face had taken back its stoic expression. "Thank you. I have to go now. Thank you."

"Will you be all right?" Marusia asked. "Shall we walk you to your house?"

"I'm fine. I'll see you good women tomorrow. *Khrystos rozhdaietsia!* Christ is born!" She left the door half open behind her, allowing a cold draft to waft inside. "Shut the door," Evdokia shouted to her remaining guest. "Don't let the ghosts in!"

Before Marusia completely closed it, the mangy stray cat rushed in. "Oh, so you followed me here," Marusia said as she bent over the animal as though to stroke it, but it ran away from her and planted itself in the middle of the kitchen, its back arched. It sniffed at the empty plates Lazorska had left on the floor.

"Get that animal out of here," Evdokia said. She hurried away from the cat, sat down at the table, and poured herself another glass of champagne. She nervously rubbed the blue and red embroidery woven into her finest linen tablecloth. "What a strange holy day this is! No empty plate—God forgive me Oleh, my husband! Lazorska going crazy here in front of us. No carolers and *vertep* actors to sing to us and bless us for a good year. No Mass. No family. *Sumno!* So depressing—so *sumno.*"

"We should at least bless the animals," said Marusia. She took a bit of herring from her plate and gently swung it in front of the cat's nose. "And since you're the only animal we have left, I bless you and thank you for your company and hope that God keeps you well in memory of the Savior's birth. And that we live for the next Christmas. Amen."

The cat ignored the fish until Marusia placed it on the floor over its bloody front paws. It grabbed the food in its torn mouth and retreated into a corner, near the chair where Oleh last sat, and struck at the sheaf of holiday wheat that was placed there.

"Oh, get that thing out of my house," Evdokia pleaded. "What a strange Christmas." She wiped her eyes with the tassled edge of the tablecloth.

"Let's finish our supper at least, and then we'll have some more of that champagne," Marusia urged. "I'll get the cat out somehow. I'll tempt him out the door with more fish."

"No, not the herring. Give it that horrible squid. I never ate such awful stuff in my life. My old man would've said something dirty about the way it's shaped," Evdokia said.

"Yes, and all that jelly it's packed in," Marusia responded. She saw that Evdokia was about to cry. "Yes, your old Oleh sure would have said something about that. He was always ready with a dirty joke."

"And what will you say, you scruffy one?" said Marusia, smiling at the cat. "This is the night when all the animals talk. Say something, and mind your manners."

The cat licked at a sore on one of its paws, then stared intently into a dark corner for a second or two before resuming its ritual.

Evdokia half smiled. "It would say, 'Thank you for a terrible Christmas. Life was better without the stupid humans when they made themselves the masters of the earth.'" Evdokia sighed. She downed the rest of her champagne, which brought a sudden brightness to her melancholy. "Hey, Marusia, look! Let's shoot some *kutia*." She scooped a large spoonful of the Christmas porridge made of wheat, poppyseeds and honey, and hurled the gluey dollop up at the ceiling. "Hah! It stuck! Means we'll have good luck this year!"

Chapter 18

THE THREE OF them survived the long, stingy winter that was unrelentless in its cold sullenness and feeble sun. At last the new spring arrived, and with it two more women: the singer Yulia Pan'kovych and her cousin, a woman named Mychailyna Shkrabanova, who had lived in another village in the zone. They had been reunited by chance at an evacuee camp near Kyiv.

The new arrivals came in the evening. They heard the church bells ringing and found their way to Evdokia's well-lit house. Lazorska and Evdokia were preparing their evening meal and welcomed them with *samohon* and soup.

"God grant you and keep you," said Yulia. Her voice was low, and her eyes were inflamed. She had lost weight, which caused the hump on her back to appear larger, but otherwise she appeared well enough. Her cousin was shorter and skinny as a broomstick. She appeared to be far younger than the others—she wore oversize modern blue-framed glasses, and she kept her babushka on tight, so that not a strand of her bushy hair could escape.

Evdokia spotted Marusia coming down the road. "Come in, come in," she yelled out the door. "We have more guests!"

Marusia was pleased to see Yulia and kissed her soft heart-shaped face. "Yulichka, you and your sweet nightingale voice returned!"

"Yes, the good Lord kept me through Stalin and Siberia and now this awful catastrophe," Yulia said, returning Marusia's damp kisses.

But Marusia halted and stepped away from her friend when she saw the other one. "You! So, out of all the good people that could have come back, God chose to spare you and lead you here to torment me."

The other woman, Mychailyna, was startled. "I didn't even think for a second that *you'd* be here. We didn't think anybody would be here."

"And why not me? I live here, not you."

"So, you know each other," Yulia broke in.

"This is the whore my husband ran off with." Marusia aimed at the legs of her rival's chair and spat on the floor.

"That's not exactly how it happened," Mychailyna whined. She had a nasal voice that was very loud, and each word was spoken with deliberate slowness. "I couldn't help it if he chose to spend the war with me."

"And the rest of his sinful life."

"But how long ago was that?" cut in Lazorska. "Really that must've been a hundred years ago."

"You didn't have to kick him out of your house. He would've come back sometime. . . . He was always married to you," Mychailyna retorted.

"He should have remembered that when he was sleeping with you!" Marusia's anger moved her physically closer to where the birdlike woman sat. She leaned over her. "So why are you here now? Why come back to Starylis? Did you expect to move into my house?" She bent lower to look at her face and was close enough to Mychailyna to see her bow-shaped lips tremble. "Did you think I was finally dead and you could just dance in and pretend you're the proper widow, you *svoloch?*"

Mychailyna coughed straight into Marusia's face. Marusia gasped as though poisoned by the intruder's breath.

"Get her some water," said Yulia, who slapped her cousin's slight back.

Marusia glared at Evdokia when she gave Mychailyna a cup of the precious Vichy water instead of the slimy brown stuff straight from the tap.

"She isn't well, Marusia," Yulia said. "And I asked her to come with me. I was too afraid to come back alone after my husband died."

"May he rest in peace," Evdokia said.

"We're all sick," grumbled Marusia. "But after forty some years, I still feel the same about this one."

"Let it rest with the dead," Lazorska said. "There are so few of us here we must get along. We could all die today."

Marusia felt betrayed by Lazorska. "That one there ruined my life! And my son's!" She turned to the little woman, who was still clearing her throat. "Are you sorry for what you did?" Marusia demanded.

Mychailyna looked up. Her eyes were magnified like an owl's through the thick lenses of her glasses. She blinked twice, and her small doll's mouth whispered, "No."

"Then you go straight to hell." Marusia slammed the door behind her and questioned God why she was always being tested in such cruel ways.

MARUSIA KEPT TO herself. She still rang the bells in the evenings but refused to participate in the communal dinners the women made together. She ignored Evdokia's visits, refusing to answer the door or to talk with her whenever Evdokia let herself in. "Don't be stupid, all men cheat," Evdokia argued at Marusia's back. "Even my Oleh. But who cared? Anyway, your man is dead. His sinning *fasol'ka* is earth now. Seeds for worms."

Yulia also tried to talk to her alone. Marusia had always liked Yulia, but her pleas that she had no idea about her cousin's past did nothing to soothe Marusia. "The less I see of her, the better we'll all get along," Marusia threatened. "Or I'll be forced to choke the life out her chicken neck quicker than any poison from Chornobyl."

Alone in her room, she rekindled her anger at her husband and cursed his name with the same venomous hurt she had felt when he first left her. In the past, so long ago, she was too young and naive to understand that he was unable to love her alone. There were always other women around—women he slept with when he worked at the *kolhosp,* women he found solace with whenever she had argued with him or demanded more attention than he wanted to give. His other women only expected a good time and found him desirable in ways she did not. But at least he never left their home, that is, not until he met that one.

That one, as Marusia called Mychailyna, *that one* was the worst of them all. She remembered too well how it happened. *That one* was younger and lived in the next village, where her father owned a bull. Antin, Marusia's husband, wanted to mate their cow. He brought the cow over to *that one's* bull, and "found himself another cow to mate," Marusia said in bitterness the few times she told anyone her troubles. "The *kham* couldn't have been more than sixteen or seventeen at the time. He was already pushing thirty and should've known better. But no, *he* was milking her and giving her the stud service," she cried out her shame.

Marusia didn't believe in divorce—to her it was a Bolshevik invention. Marriage, as miserable as it was, was still a sacrament. The last time she saw him was the torturous hour when she begged him to stay home. By then he had deserted her to live with Mychailyna at her father's house, still wearing his wedding ring. Throughout it all, she prayed that he would find his senses and return home to her and Yurko. After a year, she heard that the Red Army had found him and made him fight the Germans. The government returned his dead, shattered body to Marusia, who buried it in their family's plot in the church cemetery, complete with his victory medals and uniform.

"Why do I have to grieve him all over again?" Marusia cried before her icon. "Why am I tortured with this life of mine, Lord? Better you had left me here alone or dead."

Then she prayed that the sharpness in her heart would cease. "Oh, Lord, I'm so weak! I pick at the pain like a scab. I can't help it, Lord, I hate her so much. Help me to forgive, Lord. Or at least, help me not to care so much anymore. . . ."

LAZORSKA STOOD NEAR the doorway in the tiny vestibule of the church after Marusia finished ringing the bells.

"I haven't been here since I came back," said Lazorska. "Yulia thinks we should all come here on Sundays and sing the Mass. She will lead us."

"I'm not sure I could pray in the same room with some people," Marusia said.

"Really, you should be over it by now," Lazorska said.

"She should apologize first."

"Oh, now listen," Lazorska said. "She was young. She was foolish. It's the husband that you should blame."

"I do," Marusia retorted. "But she knew enough to make a choice between sinning and not."

"Marusia, you know she's dying."

"Who isn't around here."

"No. She's worse than ever. A lot of her hair has fallen out. She has a cancer."

"We all will die from this life's curse," Marusia said.

"Marusia, don't poison your own soul. She says she would like to see you."

"What for?" Marusia clenched her fists. "What in the world for? What the devil does she want?"

"Maybe to ask your pardon," Lazorska whispered.

"Too late! Too late! I gave her one last chance. She gave me her answer. You heard her!"

Lazorska shook her head. "Give it up," she said in a weary, spent voice.

"My life is troubled," Marusia said in a hard, even tone. "I have many crosses. I have no one left. She took my husband. My son is gone. Who knows about my grandchildren. I've seen too much death in this life. No, there's nothing I can do for her. She should ask for God's forgiveness, because I'm not able to give her any."

The women walked outside together in silence. They were almost at Lazorska's house when Marusia asked, "Are you taking care of her?"

"I gave her some potions I made up. It helps to quiet her down a bit. But she's in great pain."

"Why did she come here if she's half-dead?"

"She took care of Yulia after the explosion. Yulia's health improved, but Mychailyna grew sicker. They thought she would get better first here in Starylis, and then maybe she would go back on to her own village, but she's worse off than Yulia ever suspected."

"Why didn't Yulia just take her back to her village?"

"This was closer."

They stopped in front of Yulia's house. "I'm going in to give her another remedy," Lazorska said. "This will bring her gently to the other side. She'll have one last good sleep."

"I can't come in. I can't."

Lazorska briefly touched Marusia's shoulder and left her.

EVDOKIA CAME THE next morning to tell Marusia that Mychailyna had died quietly that night without much pain and to ask Marusia if she wanted to attend the funeral. "We'll all carry her and bury her somewhere in the churchyard. She's such a little bundle, we should do it very easily."

"I can't go." But later that day, Marusia walked alone into the churchyard and heard Yulia singing the *panakhyda* chants for the dead.

Yulia, Lazorska and Evdokia were about to break

ground in a far corner of the graveyard. Marusia called out to them, "Why are you burying her there?"

"No room. Too many dead family members in my plot," said Yulia. "It's as close as I can get to my section."

Marusia thought hard a moment. It was time to make amends with the dead, since she couldn't when her rival was alive. "No. Stop it. Bury her there. Near my husband." She pointed to another spot.

"Are you sure?" Yulia asked.

"Yes, she can have Yurko's spot. I'll be buried on the other side of them, further away, closer to my mother." She tried to swallow down some of her pain. She stood near the women and pointed a finger at them. "Remember, just bury me with something of Yurko's—his hat or his watch." Her voice cracked and her chest swelled. She turned away to lead them to her family's section.

The women took turns digging the grave, except for Marusia, who stood apart like an outsider. The earth was still partially frozen and inert from the long winter, but gradually the ground yielded and divided against their shovels. Once the grave was dug, Marusia took hold of a foot, and together the four women gently lowered the body of Yulia's cousin, Marusia's enemy, into the hole as she was, without a casket. She wore the same clothes she had on the day of her return to the village. Her head was wrapped in the same floral scarf, and her hands were clenched around an old prayer book of Yulia's. Her face looked less pinched, and her opaque eyelids were closed behind her large glasses.

The four women each threw in a handful of dirt. Marusia was especially careful not to cover the corpse's face when it was her turn. The dirt landed over Mychailyna's heart.

They finished the burial and marked her grave with a cross Evdokia had made the night before out of wood and a garland of herbs from Lazorska's garden.

Yulia grabbed Marusia's hand on the way to her house. "Thank you. You are a blessed woman."

"These things don't matter anymore," Marusia said. She turned away from Yulia, carrying the stone that still remained deep within her heart.

Chapter 19

IN THE EARLY days of April, the women realized how warm the air had become and how soft and dark the earth. "We should plant," Evdokia said one evening during a meal shared at her table. "Not only should we plant, but we need a cow. We need fresh milk," she continued in her quick-paced cadence. "I haven't had any milk since I came here. A goat would suit me fine. I had a dream last night about a goat."

"Even the evacuee camp had some milk now and then for the children and the old people," said Yulia. She declined the hard brown bread Marusia offered. "I lost two more teeth last night."

"I still think," Evdokia said, "that we should go from house to house, see what is left, and take what we need. We have so little among us."

"You can have whatever I have," said Yulia. "Lord knows, my canned vegetables look cursed and bad. I saw these evil bubbles floating around them. I didn't seal them tightly enough I suppose."

"That happens sometimes," Marusia said kindly. "Many times I canned the best of my harvests, but I forgot to seal the lids, or wash the bottles really well. The bad air pushes itself in and poof—all the good food rots."

Evdokia nodded.

"Well, you're welcome to have whatever I have left," Yulia said, her cheeks flushed. "I have some powdered milk and a sack of flour—as far as I can tell, it's still usable, although I saw a few dead worms. We can sift them out. Oh, and I found an unopened can of powdered chocolate. We can make a cake out of it, for Easter."

"Has anyone been to the village?" Lazorska asked.

No one answered.

"Our situation is not normal at all," Lazorska said. "I think it's right that we go into people's houses and take what we need."

Evdokia beamed. "Exactly! Just as I've been saying."

"Then we should only take the things we really need," Marusia said, staring at Evdokia's stolen shawl, which was torn and dirty. "Only things for an absolute emergency."

"We should keep a list of all the things we take so that when the people come back, we can find a way to barter with them or replace the food we took," Lazorska said.

"Yes, that I'll agree to," Marusia said.

"I'll keep the records," Evdokia volunteered. She pulled a notebook of graph paper out from under the short leg of a rickety table. "I'll write down whose home we visited, and what we took and how much of it."

"Fine," Lazorska said. "We need to see what the village has as well."

"Nothing in the co-op, that's for sure," Marusia said.

"But what about the post office?" Yulia asked. "I keep hoping for a letter from my son. Where would it go?"

"There's a lot of mail still in bags since the explosion," Marusia told them.

"That should be sorted out," Lazorska said. "It still belongs to people. Even if they're dead, we should sort all the mail. Later, someone might want it."

"What about the mail that we should be getting now?" Marusia asked. She was thinking that Zosia may have been trying to reach her all this time.

"The government must have our mail. In Moscow," said Lazorska.

"We should file a petition to get it," said Yulia.

"Maybe it's stuck somewhere in Chornobyl or Kyiv," said Evdokia. "The mail is always forgotten and ends up on top of someone's desk—somewhere it shouldn't have gone to."

"Well, then," said Marusia, "we have to file something official I suppose. We must go to the nearest *gorso-*

viet officials and let them know we're here. Lord knows, no one will come to us and help us." She thought of the dogcatcher and silently cursed him.

"Then let's tell them we want a cow," said Evdokia.

"Yes, my cow was about to calve when we had to leave," Marusia said heatedly. "I'm certain this poison killed her. The government should compensate me. After all, there are four of us now. When it was just me here, there wasn't anything I could do. But with four of us . . . now that's the size of an average family. That counts."

The others agreed.

"What should we do about money?" asked Evdokia. "No one is paying our pensions."

"Another declaration," said Marusia. The women laughed. "Yes, we must write to them and demand our money. It's ours."

"Let's write this document," Evdokia said, and tore a page from the notebook. "Wait, let me get one of my son-in-law's fancy pens." She searched in her daughter's old room and returned with a fountain pen and ink bottle. "So, who wants to write it?"

"Yulia, you have the most education, you know Russian best. You do it," said Marusia.

"But we all know Russian," Yulia said. "We all had to learn it."

"Yulia, you have to do it," Evdokia insisted. "It's too easy for us to make a mistake by writing one tiny Ukrainian word and spoiling the whole document."

"Yes, don't write anything in Ukrainian or they'll arrest us as bourgeoise nationalists," said Lazorska. "Worse, they'll throw it away."

"I can't write it alone," Yulia protested.

"We'll all dictate it," Lazorska said.

"Who should I address it to?" Yulia asked, scratching the pen nib on the paper to see if it would ink.

"Address it to Gorbachev," said Evdokia.

"And another to the commissar of Chornobyl," said Lazorska. "If he's still alive."

"Somebody's there. The trains run there, don't they?" Marusia said.

"Well, write to both of them," said Lazorska. "And also to the commissar of Ukraine. This will be our Village of Starylis *Ukase*."

The women spent the morning drinking tea and drafting the letter. They wrote:

> *6 April 1988*
>
> *To the Supreme President Michail Sergeyevich Gorbachev, the Supreme Commissar of the Ukrainian SSR, and the Magister of Kiev Oblast:*
>
> *We send you greetings and our wishes for your good health.*
>
> *We, the undersigned, are victims of the nuclear catastrophe at Chernobyl of 26 April 1986. Since that time, we have had to leave our homes in Starylis, give up our farm animals, endure sickness*

and hardships where we were evacuated to so far from our loved ones, and are now separated from them because many have died or have been sent to other places where we lost them.

Good Commissars, please hear our demands as we are four old and defenseless women who have always worked hard for our State. We are law-abiding citizens who are now living back in our deserted village of Starylis, and are nearly destitute. We request the following:

1. A cow. We need fresh milk. If possible, a goat and chicken or pig would also gratify us.

2. Our mail. We have not received any mail since 1986. Please send all past mail to us in Starylis—even letters for our dead or missing relatives and neighbors.

3. Our pensions. We have not received any pension money since the evacuation nor any other compensation for our having had to leave our homes and families for over a year.

4. Transportation. We need a bus or a car to take us to a nearby place where we can buy supplies or to another village where we can trade.

"Anything else?" asked Lazorska.

"I miss hearing music on the radio and television," said Yulia. "And the news. What is going on in the world?"

"Let's put in a demand for electricity and clean water," said Evdokia. So they added:

> 5. *Electricity and water. We have a little water from our wells but it is not healthy and we have no electricity at all.*

"And put in a statement about medical supplies," Lazorska offered.

"But you take care of us," Marusia said.

"My treatments can't stop this poison. We need more attention."

"What good is their medicine?" Marusia argued. "I've seen my son dying in a hospital, and nothing they had could save him. None of those tubes and wires they hooked into him like he was a lamp. Nothing helped. I would trust you sooner than have them touch me."

The others echoed Marusia's words.

"I can't save you either," Lazorska said. "I can't fight this."

"But you can help us to die," said Yulia. "You helped my cousin, God rest her soul." She glanced quickly at Marusia, who bowed her head and said nothing.

After a silence, Marusia asked, "How did Lazorska help . . . her?"

"I can only help people to die quietly."

"That's a blessing," said Evdokia. "My old man did that on his own. But I also saw so much suffering . . . especially the children."

"It's not really a sin—is it—to have help, if we have to die from this radiation poison," said Marusia. "My son suffered so much. It was a sin to keep him suffering. . . ."

"I was trained by my grandmother to make the sickness less painful whenever I could," said Lazorska. "The priests tried to get me arrested during the war for what I did. In fact, the truth be told, I *was* arrested by the *Bolsheviki* for murder. I always suspected that the priests turned on me."

"What happened?" Marusia asked.

"Everyone was denouncing everyone else then. You remember. That's how it was. You couldn't trust anyone. Then the war came and I got out, because they needed nurses. I still did what I thought was right. But only if the people I was helping wanted me to. I never did it on my own."

The women said nothing to Lazorska's confession. "Bad times, then," Yulia said, breaking the tense stillness.

"Not better now," Evdokia said. "You know, I think that when my time comes, I want to go quickly. If I'm made to suffer more than the Lord intended because man meddled in God's ways, then it's wrong for me to die in such unnatural agony—more than God Himself intended. Do you understand what I am saying? Am I a sinful woman to think this?"

"We were poisoned and not of our own doing," said Yulia. "Should we die so horribly because of man?"

"You're right," Marusia said. "We have tried to keep God's ways, but we have been forced not to. They tried to shut our churches and make us into Bolshies. They built that plant, they took away our children. They killed my son!" She rocked back and forth in her chair.

"I want to go peacefully," said Yulia. "But if I can't on my own, then will you help me, Lazorska?"

"I promise," she said.

"And me as well," said Evdokia.

"And me," Marusia said firmly.

"I promise, but you must help me when it's my time," Lazorska said.

The women nodded their heads.

"Then we don't need to say anything about medical help in our *ukase*," Evdokia declared.

Satisfied, the women signed the petition. They drew lots with the hay straws Evdokia kept on hand to light her woodstove. "The one who picks the short straw will have to walk to the Chornobyl plant and hand over our document," Marusia said. She stared at Lazorska and Yulia, whose faces were pinched in pain, then she broke the shortest one in secret and purposely held it away from those two. Evdokia also pulled a long straw.

"Well, it's up to me then," Marusia said.

"Do you want to go?" asked Lazorska. "We can draw again."

"I'll go with you," offered Evdokia.

"It fell to me, so I'll go," Marusia said. "After all, I was the first one to come back. And yes, bless you Evdokia. I'd like your company. Let's go tomorrow. Early."

They all agreed, and also decided that they wanted to examine all of the abandoned homes in case they'd forgotten something and needed to write in a last-minute addendum.

AND SO THE four women went together to each empty house. Many were locked, and those were passed over for the time when they had nothing left. "Then we can break in without feeling guilty," said Yulia.

Throughout, the women were solemn. Each house was at its own level of decay and neglect. People had left food rotting on the table, and piles of laundry hardened into lumps in the filthy washtubs, caked with the grimy residue of cheap soap. But all the villagers had stored and left behind a fine cache of food sheltered inside pantries or hidden in cellars. The women collected the bottled water and milk and other staples and put them in Marusia's wheelbarrow and in Yulia's grandchild's old brown wagon. They also took canned fish and various preserved vegetables and jams, and every item was dutifully recorded by Evdokia.

On the way to the co-op, they passed the home of old Paraskevia Volodymyrivna, the priest's mother who had kept goats.

"We didn't look in here," said Lazorska.

The house was the most rundown and forbidding in the village. The shutters were unhinged and the thatched roof was in shreds.

Lazorska stepped in and the others followed.

They were greeted by a horrible stench. In the middle of the living room floor lay the remains of two goats, their amber reptilian eyes glazed. The rug was smeared with old blood, and the fur was strewn about like clumps of dust.

"That looks like dog feces," Lazorska said. "The goats must have been attacked by wild dogs."

"I have to go out for a minute," Yulia said. The others left with her. She held on to the fence. "I needed air."

"You go on ahead and sort the food out," Lazorska called out from the doorway. "I'll clean up as best as I can, get some of the stink out. Then I'll see what she had."

"Why bother?" said Evdokia. "She won't come back. She probably didn't have much anyway."

"She was my friend. She loved those goats."

The women halfheartedly offered to help, but Lazorska insisted she could do it alone. "I don't mind. But go ahead and get the store organized. I'll meet you later."

They were glad to escape Paraskevia's sad home and to have time for organizing the store, which took up most of the day. The women found that the villagers' supplies would easily fill up all the co-op shelves in full view. Evdokia left the notebook on the countertop. "If we need anything, all we have to do is sign it out and this way we won't have to bother one another all the time," Evdokia said. It was her idea for everyone to use the honor system.

Lazorska had not shown up by the time they were finished, so Marusia suggested that they go to the post office and sort out the mail.

"I haven't been here since my first time back," she said. They decided that since Yulia would be leading church services, and Lazorska was of course the healer, and Evdokia in charge of the co-op, then Marusia should be the postmistress. "Remember, you're still in the Soviet Union and have to work, work, work," Evdokia teased, but became quiet when no one laughed along with her.

The women were more somber in the post office than in the store. Lenin's faded portrait looked down on them as they hauled the sacks to the center of the dusty floor and poured out bundles of mail at a time. There was nothing postmarked after April 1986. Between the three of them, they sorted the mail according to families and bundled it with the string and remnants of rope they found buried in drawers that hid stamps and an abacus with black wooden beads. Then they shoved all the mail that fit into pigeonholes and piled the rest on the countertop.

"Look, here's a letter for you," Yulia said to Evdokia. It was addressed to Hanna in care of her grandmother.

Evdokia stared at it. It was a postcard with a picture of a deep blue ocean. Square white granite hotels were prominent in the background. On the other side was a greeting wishing the newlyweds good luck. "That's from my husband's nephew's family in Odesa. They couldn't send a real wedding present, oh, no. I'm surprised they bothered to write at all."

Marusia found an envelope addressed to Zosia. "Well, here's one for my family." She felt odd. It couldn't be from Zosia's mother because the return address wasn't from Siberia. Her stomach tightened. She searched for a more recent letter from Zosia, but none had come for her.

It was early evening before they were through with the mail. Lazorska was not in sight. Yulia stood up and stretched. "I'm going over to help Lazorska."

Evdokia walked with her, but Marusia lingered in the post office. She wanted to be alone for a few minutes. She had to open the letter. The envelope was made of faint pink linen paper. She liked the way it felt, elegant and rich. The handwriting looked practiced and large, almost like Katia's but less childish. She had to open the letter. The letter was written on typical graph paper stationery. Here, the ink strokes were larger and angrier. In Russian it said:

> *Stay away from my husband or I will have to tell the authorities. I will also tell your husband. Forget about trying to make him to marry you. He's only using you, and will never leave me. He said that to me himself. For your own good, and his and mine, leave him. He has a wife and his own children. Leave him alone.*

She couldn't make out the scribbled signature. It looked like Liena, or Genya, maybe Nina. Who is that? she wondered.

She thought about it and then was glad she didn't know. She was relieved that Yurko didn't know about this. Or did he? She thought about Zosia and Yurko and their lives together. Why couldn't they have been happy? He was like me, she thought, unlucky in the people he loved.

She tore up the letter and hid the pieces in her dress pocket. It was too stupid—all of that, so unnecessary. Life passes too quickly for such nonsense. Marusia was surprised to suddenly feel a bolt of remorse for Zosia. Zosia was unlucky, too, and Marusia felt tremendous grief for all of the lost chances she might have taken to try for an understanding, an alliance of respect with her strong-willed daughter-in-law. And it was too late for that as well.

She would burn the pieces in her stove later. Now she hurried to see what damage was left to be cleared from Paraskevia Volodymyrivna's house before it was time to ring the bells.

Chapter 20

MARUSIA AND EVDOKIA planned to leave early in the morning for their walk to Chornobyl, but even before daylight they were awakened by shouts of obscenities and a rumbling motor shattering the still night.

"Oh, no—not another explosion." Marusia sat up and searched in the dark for her slippers. She lit a candle and hurried to her window. The sky was a soft dark blue. There were several hours before the first tentacles of morning light. She couldn't see anything unusual, so she put on a shawl, grabbed her crowbar from the woodstove, and went outside. The air was cool and smelled of springtime. She didn't see any stars through the hazy clouds, but could make out the outer scythelike rim of the half-moon poking through. She followed the noise down the path to the church.

"Marusia, is that you?" hissed Evdokia from her

open window. "Hey!" she yelled, tapping the pane a few times, but Marusia didn't hear her over the din. "Wait for me!" She ran and caught Marusia passing her gate. Marusia hardly recognized her friend, who had her gray hair plaited into two braids that bounced over her plump breasts. "What is that noise?" Evdokia asked, breathless.

"I don't know. A tractor?" They stopped at Lazorska's yard, where she stood rigid in the middle of the road, her arms crossed. She was dressed in her usual black dress and scarf.

"*Woch!* Lazorska, it's you," Evdokia gasped. "I thought you were a night spirit. Some kind of mean *Lisovi* ghost come to take me away. Yoy!"

Yulia had also been awakened and came out to join the other women. She carried an ax. "Good idea," Evdokia whispered. She searched the misty ground for a thick stick for herself in case they had to defend themselves. The women walked down past the churchyard and onto the path that led to the *kolhosp.* In the thin slice of moonlight, they could see the outlines of two people and half a car.

"Be careful," Lazorska cautioned. "We don't know what they're doing or who they are."

Marusia blew out her candle. The two figures seemed unaware of the women who crept along behind the bushes and beneath the canopies of shadowy trees in the dark. When they were close enough to hear one of them, a young man, swear loudly, they realized he was working beneath the hood of a car. He lifted up his face in clear view to the group. A large case of tools, a pickax and two shovels were on the ground.

"Hold it, Oles!" he yelled to his friend who was in the car revving the engine. "Who are you?" the young boy demanded of the stunned women. "Are you *gorsoviet* agents? Listen, we weren't doing anything."

Evdokia spoke up. "Hey, is that you, Mykola Hnatsenko?" His friend stumbled out of the car. They both stared stupidly at the women. "Don't you know me, you little fool? I'm Hanna's grandmother." Evdokia turned to the other women. "You should all know this crazy child. Let me introduce you to Mykola. 'Mykola-*shkoda*' we called him because he wasted his life. One of Hanna's old boyfriends from the plant. What are you doing here? I thought you left to live in Chornobyl a few years back."

The young man smiled, showing a mouthful of steel teeth. He had deep pockmarks on his hairless young cheeks, and his blond hair fell over his dull green eyes. "Oh, sure. Evdokia Zenoviivna. How are you?"

"Never mind that. What are you doing here in the middle of the night?"

His friend Oles, a taller boy with darker hair, cut in. "We could ask you that. What are *you* doing here? This is a dead zone. No one is supposed to be here."

"Well, how about that, because as you can see, we're here in the flesh and blood shivering in our nighties. We live here," retorted Evdokia.

"We came back from the evacuation," Marusia put in.

"So, there's people here now?" asked Mykola.

"Just us," Evdokia said.

"Just the four of you?" Oles laughed. He poked My-kola in the ribs with his elbow. "So, you're not really sup-posed to be here? Great! Just old ladies! That's great! Nothing to worry about, Kolya."

"Wait one minute," Marusia said. She didn't like their disrespectful tone, especially from that puppy Oles. "We came back. This is our home. I don't know either of you boys. You're not here to live with us, are you? It doesn't look like you're moving in anywhere. So, what are you doing here in the middle of God's immortal night?"

"Look," Oles said, "why don't you go back to sleep and forget you saw us. We'll be out of here soon and you lovely beauties can all live here happily ever after." The boys laughed.

In low voices, the women murmured among themselves. Then Marusia stepped closer to the car. "How do you know that we're not supposed to be here? We *babysi* are everywhere, in every government office, on every hotel floor, on every street corner cleaning, working night and day. We are the eyes and ears of the government. Now suppose I tell my boss, whose name you would know quicker than your own fathers', about what you bad little boys are doing here in the middle of a dead zone." Marusia walked around the car and tapped the hood with her crowbar. "Whose car is this?"

"Yes, whose car?" Evdokia played along. She had

never liked Mykola anyway. "I don't remember you ever making enough money to have a car. They kept giving you the lousiest jobs and firing you because you were no good. No wonder my Hanna married someone else—a top Communist official. So, let's see some proof that it belongs to you and not to the people!"

Lazorska feebly kicked the back tires that were half mired in the dirt. A mound of earth was piled next to the automobile. "I see what's going on here," she declared. "After everyone left, you buried someone else's car. Now you're stealing it."

"Oh boys, that's thirty years in Perm for you," said Yulia. "Believe me, I know. Next stop . . . Siberia."

"That's an official deputy's car for sure," said Evdokia.

"Then it's fifty years, and after that ten more just to prove that you can't get away with it," Yulia said.

The boys looked nervous. Oles lit a cigarette and Mykola scratched his face. "So," Marusia said, "does this monster work?"

"We got it out as far as it would go," Mykola said in a respectful tone. "But it still needs work. We've got to dig it out some more."

"I'm sure you can do that, you're such strong boys," said Marusia with more confidence. "Then you will take us to the *gorsoviet* in Chornobyl. We have an important document to deliver—something to the *magister.*"

"Look, *babo,* I'm not taking you anywhere," Oles shouted. "This is my car. Prove that it isn't. I don't care if you call the authorities on me, but I'm getting out of this area. I'm not going to Chornobyl."

Marusia thought of Zosia and what she would have said if she were here. She wasn't going to back down. She planted herself directly in front of the boys. "Listen you little ball of snot. I didn't put up with all the catastrophes in my life—the war and then the explosion —for me in my old age to be yelled at by a piece of duck shit like you. You *will* take me to Chornobyl when you get this car working again! I don't care if it takes six months. I will sit myself down like this—" She poked a hole in the ground with the crowbar. "—right on this same grass I myself drove a tractor over. And I will watch you day and night until I hear that car roar. I have to get a cow for us. Then you'll bring me back here to the village. After *that,* you can run off in this junk heap and take the devil for a joyride for all I care." She thought a second as to how the cow would fit in this car, but she let that pass for now because her mind was set on getting her way.

"Good for you, Marusia," cheered Evdokia. Lazorska turned her head to the side and let out a cackle. Yulia raised her ax above her head and waved it in the air.

Mykola glanced at his friend. "Oh, take her, what the hell."

"And besides," coaxed Evdokia, "there's six of us all together. We could help you push the car out of the pit."

"All right," said Oles. "Let's just get on with it."

It was another two hours before Oles could get the

dead engine alive and sputtering into a reliable, steady hum. The women helped push, rock, and heave it out of the dirt. Before the boys could run off, Yulia, still clutching her ax, sat down in the backseat of the car with Lazorska, while Marusia and Evdokia returned to their homes to change their clothes and collect some food for the road.

"Do you have the *ukase?*" Lazorska asked as she and Yulia relinquished their seats.

"Yes, right here." Marusia patted her chest.

"If you please, ladies, let's go," Oles said, holding the passenger-side door open. Marusia and Evdokia climbed into the back and held the ends of their babushkas over their noses to keep from sneezing. Luckily, the boys or whoever buried the car had thought to shut the windows before it was completely filled with dirt.

MARUSIA AND EVDOKIA were jostled during the short, bumpy ride, but held on to the short leather straps over the windows. The car slowed down near the plant's gates. Oles stared at the rearview mirror. "Look, we have to let you off here. We can't wait around."

"Honest, we're in deep trouble as it is," pleaded Mykola.

"Shut up," Oles said.

"I'm sorry, ladies," Mykola said. "But someone's looking for me. We've got to go. Otherwise, they'll make me clean up the radiation. . . ." Mykola turned to look at the old women. "Honest, I'm sorry. But please let us go. We kept our end. We just can't wait for you or take you back."

"That's all right, son," Marusia said. "Thank you and good luck."

"Say hello to your mother for me," said Evdokia to Mykola. She ignored the other one.

Once the women had gotten out of the car, it spun crazily around and sped out of sight.

"Well, at least we only have to walk one way," said Evdokia. "We can lead the cow, if we get one. I've done that a million times in my life."

The women stood in front of the high fence that surrounded the Chornobyl plant. They weren't sure where to go, or even how to get inside.

They approached the main gate, where a Red Army guard stopped them.

"Halt!" he yelled. "This is restricted territory. You are not allowed to go further!" He stormed toward them with his rifle cocked and aimed.

"Please, *tovaryshi,*" Marusia said. "We come on business. We're from Starylis."

"You can't be from there," the guard said. He was young, with pimples on his broad babyface. "There are no residents in the zone areas, except for authorized personnel."

"We're from Starylis," Marusia repeated, trying to sound calm. "There are two more women in our village besides us. We came to speak to the *magister.*"

"We want a cow," Evdokia blurted out. "Please."

"Are you spies?" he asked.

Evdokia giggled nervously. "Who wants to know?" she said.

"*Ssh*." Marusia was frightened. He might be crazy enough to shoot them where they breathed. He made them lift up their arms in the air, and with one hand searched them, causing dust to puff out from their threadbare clothing each time he patted them.

"Look, son, we're evacuees," Marusia said after he was through. "Our sons and daughters worked here before the explosion. Now some of us old ones have come back. We're here to tell someone official and to get a cow."

"What the hell is going on here, Officer Rostov?" said a thick, dark voice. A man dressed in a suit and tan trench coat stepped out of a new-model Soviet-built black Volga and strode up to them. "Why are you attacking these women? Did you have another fight with your mother-in-law and are declaring war against all the *babysi* now?"

"Sir." The guard saluted the man in the trench coat, then resumed pointing the rifle at the women. "They said they're from the zone, sir. But no one's there. They could be spies."

"Oh, put that idiotic thing away," said the man. His voice was coated with whiskey. "Damn *Svejk*. Ever read *Good Soldier Svejk*? No? Great book. This idiot is the adopted son. Now what is this all about? Please, ladies, put your arms down."

"We came here to see the *magister,*" Marusia said.

The man laughed. "Damn if that isn't precious! Damn!"

"Show him the *ukase,*" Evdokia nudged. Marusia modestly took the document from inside the front of her dress and handed it to the man in the trench coat.

He laughed harder. "Damn! And to Gorbachev, too. You old women are amazing. And this fool wanted to shoot you. Come with me! This is too good to miss!"

The women were humbled more by the man's exuberance than by the guard's rifle. And they were awed by the plant itself—a busy place with people in white and brown jumpsuits milling around, many saluting the man who walked briskly and a little ahead of the women.

Marusia and Evdokia glanced nervously out of the sides of their eyes at the red and white towers that loomed atop massive concrete buildings. Behind those stood a decrepit structure that looked as though a fire had gutted it. It was crowned with a black carapace. "A church painted black?" Marusia whispered to Evdokia, who shrugged. Marusia quickly crossed herself in tiny circular movements so as not to be noticed.

They were taken to a building farther away from the gate, and into an office where several pretty women were typing mysterious messages at large, bulbous computer terminals.

Then they were led into another office where a fat little man—Marusia thought he might be the ghost of Nikita Khrushchev—sat behind a small desk without anything on it except an ink stand and a magazine opened to pages with bright pictures of skiers on mountaintops. He was about to sip a steaming glass of tea when the man in the trench coat ushered the women in.

"Ladies, this is the *magister*. Tell him everything you told me."

The women were asked to sit down.

"Please, *tovarishch*," Marusia said. "If you don't mind we'll stand. We're dirty from our journey." She didn't want to smudge the clean white plastic chairs.

The man in the trench coat gave the fat man the *ukase*. "Read this! It's wonderful!"

The *magister* shook his head. "Unbelievable." Marusia could see he wasn't as amused by it as the other man. "But why did you women come back? Who gave you permission?"

"We read in the newspaper that only thirty-one people died from the accident, and that now things were back to normal, and so we wanted to come home to die. We lost our families and we have no money. So, we want our homes. . . ." Marusia's voice trembled and faltered.

"And a cow," Evdokia said.

"Well, we have to inspect this more closely," the *magister* said, flustered. He cleared his throat. "Well, go on back now . . . wherever you are living. Where was it?"

"In Starylis, *tovarishch*," Marusia said.

"Well, that's not really allowed," he said. His forehead suddenly burst with oily droplets of sweat. "Really, not allowed. I'll have to take that up with the committee as well."

"Excuse me please, but where are we supposed to live, then?" Marusia said. "We have nowhere to go."

The *magister* thumped his thick hairy fist on his desk. "You can be arrested for inhabiting a forbidden zone," he shouted.

"Sasha, Sashen'ko," the trench coat cut in. "They have a point. Where would they go? Unless you and your lovely Masha put them up in your apartment. Now, that's a good idea! What do you say? A couple of beauties here and the devil knows who else is lurking around under their beds in their village. They can cook for you, bake bread, comb your hair. . . ."

"Not a funny joke, Dmitri Pavlovych," the *magister* hissed at his crony.

"Well, then I'll take them home with me. My place needs a good scrubbing since my wife left me. Do you ladies know how to make a good cheesecake? I haven't had that in a long time. Maybe I need a cow, too, Sasha. . . ."

"Enough!" the *magister* said. "You women—how many did you say are in the village there?" He was staring at Evdokia, who was openly smiling at him.

"Four of us," Marusia answered. She was annoyed at Evdokia's unusual muteness.

"What makes you think that you are above the law of the people's government and you can live anywhere you want?"

Marusia wanted to be as convincing as Zosia would have been. She needed to choose her words carefully, in Russian—otherwise it would be so easy for this Khrushchev impostor to dismiss them, or worse, send them to a jail as spies or for that catchall anti-Soviet crime of hooliganism.

"But *tovarishch*," Marusia said carefully, reaching into her bag for her internal passport with the heavily embossed hammer and sickle emblem on the red cover. "You'll see that my passport says that I am and always have been a resident of Starylis. Even in Kiev, I tried to find a place after my son died in a hospital, but they never gave me a home. He worked for the plant here. He was an engineer, and a Young Pioneer and a Party member, too. I myself worked nearly all of my life on the collective farm, and my husband served and died in the Great Patriotic War. . . ." What else could she say? Marusia thought wildly. So far, the *magister* sat there glaring at her. The smirking man in the trench coat yawned. She swallowed and continued.

"We are old women who have never been anywhere except on the land the government let us use to live on. For which we are grateful. We only ask that you in Soviet brotherhood and friendship continue to protect us and let us live our last few years in good citizenship for our *Soyuez* by giving us a cow—at least." There, that sounded patriotic enough, Marusia thought. She nudged Evdokia to echo her words, but Marusia saw that the *nunya* merely nodded her head and smiled like a fool at the two men.

"Well, this is highly unusual," the *magister* said. He wiped his perspiring face with the thin paper napkin that was placed under his tea glass and gazed at his cohort. "What the devil am I supposed to do with these *babysi?*" he whispered to the other man.

The trench coat leaned down toward the *magister*'s shiny bald pate and whispered, "Listen, this could be great publicity for us. It would prove that people can come back. And," he said in a lower tone, "they're old anyway. Hell, they'll be gone soon enough. If we tell *Pravda* about how we're taking care of the people and leak it to the West, we'll look better for it. Give them a damn cow. What the hell!"

"And our pensions, please," Marusia said.

"And our other requests, please," Evdokia finally spoke out.

"Well," said the fat man, pulling on one of his thick eyebrows. "The cow is, of course, something you should have. We'll get you one soon. As for the rest, I'll take it up with my committee."

"Thank you, good sir," said Evdokia, clasping her hands and shaking them in front of her in a gesture of thanks. She turned and headed for the door.

Marusia didn't want to have come so far and not have anything to show for it. She didn't trust the fat stupid man nor his laughing partner. She gingerly sat down on the edge of the white chair. "We need a cow, now. We haven't had milk or cheese or butter for over a year." She tilted her chair forward toward the *magister*.

His wide face stared blankly at Marusia.

"Oh, give them a damn cow," the trench coat said. "Come on, Sasha. What do you care?"

"Oksana," the *magister* bellowed. A middle-aged woman with big worried eyes behind huge pink-rimmed glasses hurried in. "Does Pripyat have any cows to spare? A milking one."

MARUSIA AND EVDOKIA returned to the village in a pickup truck arranged by the plant. In the back, a skinny but live cow was tethered for them. On the way from the outskirts of Prypiat' where they found the cow, the driver teased the women that its calf was born with two heads. "I can't believe such a thing," Evdokia said with scorn.

"Have it your way," he chuckled. The three of them pushed the cow into Marusia's small shed, where her old cow once lived.

That night the women drank warm fresh milk, which was sweet enough for their hunger. No one mentioned how wan the cow looked or how mangy its fur. No one laughed at the slight blue tinge of its hooves, or at the way it mooed, like a broken siren.

Chapter 21

ON THE SECOND anniversary of the explosion, the women wore black armbands they tore from old pieces of cloth. They took turns ringing the bells for a total of thirty-one times in memory of the official count of the dead. But when they were finished, they seemed unable to stop. They knew the catastrophe had stolen more souls than that, and so the ringing continued far past thirty-one.

In the evening, the women gathered together and Yulia sang the *panakhyda* inside the church. They lit candles and made a solemn procession around the church and into the graveyard, where they finished their prayers.

Their Easter celebration earlier in the month had been barely more joyous. Marusia made a *paska* from the flour Yulia donated and from the precious powdered egg mixture Evdokia had found in one of her neighbors' homes.

Evdokia, for her part, gave Marusia a cup and a half full of dried raisins and generous handfuls of candy sprinkles she had used in the past to adorn her own Easter bread. They shared a simple loaf, which turned out lumpy and tasted of too much flour in the dough because Marusia refused to use the bottled water that would have made the bread lighter.

Marusia grated her fresh horseradish root into a batch of her best new beets, which were a faded red color when she boiled and peeled away their leathery black skins. Disappointing, but it had to do for the holy day.

This Easter, they wouldn't have a ham, but Lazorska was able to churn butter from the cow's cream, and Yulia shaped the butter into a lamb, an odd custom she'd learned from a Polish prisoner in the camps.

Yulia also found a nest full of blue robin's eggs in the graveyard, and she wanted to collect them and decorate them as *pysanky*—traditional elaborately decorated eggs—because, as she reminded the others, "You know the saying—*pysanky* hold all the evil between the lines we draw on the eggshells, and that way the world will continue." The eggs smelled odd, as though the unhatched birds were already stillborn. She pierced a hole in one of the eggs with a sewing needle and tried to blow out the yolk. A gray, putrid fluid flowed out. "Maybe next year we'll have some proper chicken eggs," she reasoned. She threw the egg out into the field with great force, and afterward she could not lift her arm without a stab of pain.

Together the women attended church for the Easter service and blessed their paltry baskets with holy water before going to Evdokia's house for the holiday breakfast. Their meal was morose. The women were wearied by their lives, and they had little compensation for their futures. They ate their disappointing food quietly, drank their fifty-gram shots of aged home-brewed *horilka,* and recalled the Resurrection in their toasts. No one had the heart to liken their situation to a rebirth, no one dared say that the four of them sitting together in somber anxiety was a miracle. "More like the Last Supper than an Easter breakfast," Evdokia grumbled. She was the only one who ate the powdered chocolate cake that tasted bitter and crumbled into pieces on their meager table.

THE SPRING TURNED into another humid summer, and the women tended their gardens. Lazorska was busy trying to revitalize her medicinal shrubs, but many of the plants and herbs were too withered to grow or had altogether disappeared from the garden. "This earth is too sick for my healing plants," she joked.

At summer's end, they decided to chop down some birch trees for the coming winter. They wanted to stack the wood so that it would dry in time for the frosts. Yulia winced at the work. She had spent her youth doing this work in exile in Siberia and could feel her strength diminishing. Her limp was worse, and her arm was stiff with pain. Still, she refused to ask the others for help and wanted to cut her own wood. Trying to pull down an old rotted tree by using leather straps she tied to her chest and waist, she collapsed and couldn't move. She managed to heave herself up and drag her twisted body to her kitchen. There, she crumpled and lay on the floor until Evdokia and Marusia found her the next day.

Yulia was dying—it showed in her thin face, which folded into pain whenever she coughed up gobbets of warm, dark blood. She lingered for three days before she asked Lazorska to take her away.

Early that morning, Marusia woke up to find a worn Lazorska sitting on her doorstep. "We had to let another go," she said, concentrating on the sun that was mating with the morning clouds.

Evdokia was the most sorrowful over Yulia. "I hoped I'd go first so that she could sing for me."

The funeral was still and quiet, because no one had the heart to sing without Yulia's voice.

WHEN EVDOKIA'S TURN came, she would not go without a fight. Evdokia had caught pneumonia harvesting her squash and potatoes in the early fall. The squash vines were especially hearty and blooming when she fell over in her patch and could not stop gasping. Marusia happened to have seen her bent over her garden on her way from ringing the church bells. "*Koo-koo!* Hey, did you find a man you are going to reject and give a squash to?" Marusia called out to her friend. It was a folk custom for a woman to give a suitor a squash if she rejected his love. When Evdokia didn't answer, Marusia ran to her and half carried her friend into the house.

Evdokia's condition grew worse, but she survived and with great will lingered most of the difficult winter. Marusia had moved in, and she and Lazorska tended her.

Gradually, Evdokia grew less interested in her own life and slept without the aid of the dried hops Marusia brewed for her in teas. She had turned a jaundiced yellow and lost weight. With her high fevers, she often hallucinated. Other times she was lucid. In the middle of a great frost that winter, Evdokia complained in a clear voice that her skin was about to explode and begged to be taken away. Marusia ran down the road to call for Lazorska, who followed her and brought with her the sack of forbidden medicines.

Marusia watched as Lazorska caressed Evdokia's head and spoke quiet, soothing words to calm her fears. "It will be fine," she whispered.

"I'm so afraid," Evdokia gasped out. Her face glistened with sweat. Marusia blessed her with holy water. Lazorska gave her a root herb mixed with spearmint and valerian to chew on, then a drink that smelled of sweet almonds. Evdokia slept hard, her breathing dropping to shallow wisps.

Lazorska and Marusia were with her when Evdokia quietly sighed her last breath. The three held each other's hands until Evdokia's grew cold. Before the women left, Marusia placed Oleh's pipe on Evdokia's still chest.

The winter dragged on for the last two women, who made sure to see each other at least once a day, although they had little to say. Marusia liked to visit the new graves alone so she could think about her two dead friends—not the way they were in the last miserable months of old age and torment, but when they were all young together. Yulia had been a tall, dark girl with a loud booming voice that drowned out the choir at church. She was an athlete, too—always running away from the boys who tried to catch her around the waist. Her long, wavy hair had a way of coming undone in the wind. And Evdokia—Marusia's best school friend. They had liked the same boys, shared their silly girlish secrets and squabbles together, and were inseparable until Marusia married. Evdokia never liked Antin. "And you were right about him, you bossy one," Marusia said, smiling through her sadness. "I should've listened to you, my friend. I wish I could hear you now."

Marusia kept busy canning what she could, including Evdokia's squash, which she boiled and strained but, out of grief, simply couldn't bring herself to eat.

Chapter 22

ANOTHER SPRING CAME, bringing the welcome trickle of water from the icicles that had formed beneath the roof eaves and were melting away in the warming sun. Yellow crocuses and snowdrops grew strong and hearty in the snow. Thin shrills of young birds were heard on the budding trees, and Marusia brushed a new caterpillar off a dead oak.

More people came back. Some returned because they had read a story in *Pravda* about villagers returning to the zone. When their patience was worn through by the deaths of families and the sorrow of lost homes, many of the older former Starylis villagers returned home. Almost all of them were welcomed by Marusia's bell ringing when they arrived. By the end of May, the village had grown to a community of fifteen people.

Marusia was only too happy to have them come and take over the duties of the co-op and the post office.

She was relieved to return the foodstuffs to their rightful owners and to hand out the rest of the old mail to the survivors. From them she heard their stories and learned about what had happened to the others she once knew and who would never be seen on earth again. Unfortunately, no one had any news about Zosia or the children.

At last, the mail was coming through to Starylis again. With the others, Marusia visited the post office once a week when the mail truck stopped by. She was always disappointed. She never received any word from Zosia. Someday she would, she hoped. The government had mailed her some of her pension, but she felt too weak and weary to attempt another trip to the *magister* for the rest of her lost money. "Maybe somebody else could handle such matters," she told herself. "I can't fight anymore."

The church doors reopened, another priest came, and the entire Mass was sung every Sunday morning. But Marusia kept her custom of ringing the bells more in memory of the dead and because it eased her soul. All of the newcomers replanted their gardens, and a few of the stronger ones cultivated and harvested some sections of the *kolhosp*. They were intent on selling their new crops into the cities, just as before.

Still, each survivor suffered from ailments that were blamed on the radiation. Lazorska did all she could when she could be found. As time passed, she kept more and more to herself and grew thinner and quieter, and gradually, fewer people sought her skills.

Only one death occurred that summer among the returnees, and it was one that was not related to the poison. Ivan Avramenko tried to repair old Paraskevia Volodymyrivna's ruined roof because he thought he would live there instead of in his own much smaller house. He fell off a ladder that wobbled away from the side of the building and broke his neck. After that, Paraskevia Volodymyrivna's house was considered cursed and was left to rot.

In late summer, Marusia noticed that the mosquitoes nipped her again, and that normal butterflies were feasting hungrily on sunflower heads. Blueberries grew in robust abandon alongside the dirt roads, and all the returnees except for Marusia had a proliferation of cabbage heads blossoming in their gardens. Her cow did well enough, but it was obvious that one cow—and a motley one at that—could not feed the entire village, and some of the new arrivals petitioned for more cows. The hay field was threshed, and the clover grew back on the green land. Three more cows were soon grazing in the fields. Another miracle was evident when a few storks returned to nest on the roofs of some of the reoccupied homes.

On the morning of the feast day of the Transfiguration, the cat that had kept Marusia company for so long was found dead on her front step. She hadn't seen it for a long time, but she recognized its crooked body. "So you did want me to bury you after all," she murmured. "That's why you're here." She took an old shawl, wrapped the cat in it, and buried it near her yard. She felt lonely for the forlorn animal, although she remembered how sullen and unfriendly it had become before it abandoned her completely.

The cat's little funeral made her melancholy. Marusia's thoughts floated to Lazorska, whom she hadn't seen for over two weeks. She decided to visit her after she'd rung the bells.

But when she knocked on Lazorska's door, there was no answer. Marusia let herself in and found a dark room that was crowded with old potted plants on the shelves and tables all dying from lack of water and care. Dried herb posies veiled in cobwebs hung upside down on the low ceiling beams.

Lazorska sat at her table near two long windows that overlooked her once beautiful, abundant garden, now unkempt and grown over.

Marusia tapped the healer gently on the shoulder and was relieved to see her look up, but was surprised by how gaunt and cavernous her face had become. "I'm glad you're here," Lazorska said in a high-pitched voice that wasn't her own. "My time is coming. I don't know how much longer I can stand this. . . ." She pushed herself closer to Marusia. "God should've taken me already."

She smiled a crooked grin, exposing gaps where her fine white teeth had once been. Her jaw was extended, and her skin was a thin sheath over her protruding cheekbones. *"Samohon?"* she said, nodding slightly to a bottle with clear liquid on a shelf. Marusia took it down, poured two small ceramic cups full, and placed one in Lazorska's clawlike hand. She drank it, spilling most of it down her mouth and throat before dropping the cup. Marusia picked it up, filled it again, and raised it to her friend's gray lips.

"You, too," Lazorska whispered. Marusia raised her cup in silence to her friend, then drank it up.

"There are some gladioli bulbs I saved for you. And hollyhocks," Lazorska said. She wiped her mouth. "There —on the table, next to the other things."

Marusia found the bulbs. "These?" she asked, her eyes on the brown bottle she had watched Lazorska pour from for Yulia and Evdokia. She understood what her friend wanted from her.

"Thank you. I'll plant them so that we can have flowers in the church."

"Plant them soon," Lazorska whispered. "Plant them so you can see them soon." Her eyes were glazed with tears. "Marusia, I've been afraid for my death. What if it was a sin?" She grabbed Marusia's hand and hooked herself to her. "What if what I did all those years was a sin? What happens to my mortal sinful soul if I do it myself and I roast in hell next to all the ones I killed? That's why I can't do it to myself. What is next for me?" Lazorska's thin, humped shoulders shook. She released Marusia's hand and dropped her head on the table.

"Listen to me—I will take it on my soul," Marusia said. "You did nothing but good in this life. You've helped the sick and dying ones. Now, let me help you. I take it on my soul. Let me end your suffering like I promised. Let me help you face God."

Marusia waited until Lazorska finished her silent prayers, and then she kissed her friend's thin face that always reminded her of spun linen—smooth and cool and imprinted with the faint marks of fine lines woven into her flesh for strength.

Chapter 23

ON THE MORNING of Marusia's last day in life, the air was dry and the sun's scorching rays beat hammers on the top of everyone's head. Even the farm animals' tongues hung out of their mouths like dowsing sticks in the grass, twitching for invisible water.

The air steamed. Marusia was unable to thoroughly drench her garden because her well was running dry. She took her watering can and sprinkled the browning plants, but the water wasn't enough for their thirst. "Even my tears are dried up," she moaned.

She had to get out of the garden. Her head was soaked beneath her babushka, and she was dizzy. The last few weeks she had been unusually light-headed and in constant pain—every joint ached, and the insides of her eyelids felt like sandpaper scraping the last bit of moisture from her sore red eyes. Her body felt hot and inflamed, not only from the heat, but from some internal source that fired every pore in her skin, worse than a rash that wouldn't heal.

She needed to feel better and took out a bottle of *samohon* from the kitchen cabinet. She sat at her table, where she filled a fifty-gram shot glass full. The strong drink burned a glow in her chest and made her feel hotter. She wiped the sweat from off her eyebrows and above her upper lip and tried to finish the drink, but her hands trembled and she felt nauseated from its gasoline smell.

She sat down and took from her pocket a wad of her black hemp gum and slowly chewed it soft with the nubs of the few teeth she had left in front. Lately, so many of her back teeth, even the silver ones, had fallen out, and her gums had swelled and turned dark, thick, red and fleshy, like the inside of a plum. The drug made her feel calmer and not quite as hot.

Two days earlier she had started to clean her house. She found the old suitcase she had taken to Kyiv. It stood dormant, wedged between large round bottles of fruit compote made and sealed years ago. In her solitary grief, she had not been able to unpack the suitcase since her return to Starylis.

Now she had an enormous desire to open it. She wheezed and coughed her way to the pantry, knelt on the dusty floor, and dragged it loose from its hiding place. She sprang open the lock and looked inside. One by one, she took out the bulky items she had wrapped so long ago in inky newspaper—the few clothes that she had taken to Kyiv: a flannel nightgown, a pair of woolen stockings. Inside a sock, she found Yurko's wedding ring, the plain gold band she'd been given by the nurses after he died. In the matching sock, she found his watch. It read 2:30. She put it on her wrist. The last item was a striped shirt of Yurko's that he had never had a chance to wear. She sighed and put all of the things, except for the watch, back inside the suitcase.

Marusia dipped into the deep blue satin pouch that hung inside the suitcase. She was surprised when she found the white lace hair ribbon Katia wore. In that awful hospital basement in Kyiv, Katia had thrown it down after she caught Tarasyk putting it on his head.

And then, in her dizziness, she found Tarasyk's blond curls—fine strands, gentle as clouds, she thought. She feverishly kissed the ribbon and the hair. Marusia wove the ribbon through a buttonhole of her dress and kept the curls inside one of her fists.

"Oy! Okh! Too much," she groaned. She stood up and thought that she should water her garden, or at least hoe and weed the crops. No time to cry. So overgrown, she thought. *Han'ba!* Shameful! I'll starve if I don't save the garden.

The weeds ruled, crowding out the good crops faster than she had the strength to chop them back. She went out again into the garden and thought that the cow must need water, too, but . . . had the pitiful animal died a week ago, or was it grazing on the *kolhosp* land? She couldn't remember.

Marusia sat down on the step outside. She shaded her eyes from the harsh glare and tried to make out the figure in the garden, near the empty cowshed. A golden figure—an angel—was sprinkling her garden with her watering can. The angel's back was toward Marusia, but she saw its shoulder-length golden hair lift away from its head when a cool breeze picked up—little tufts of hair floating away like dandelion seeds. The hair swirled on the ground around Marusia's feet. It glowed and shimmered on the earth, and she thought of the gold painted on icons.

"I have some, too," she said, and released Tarasyk's hair into the gentle cascade of soft wind that surrounded her head. It danced higher and higher until she had to shut her eyes because the sunlight dazzled and blinded her.

"Don't leave me," she murmured, then nodded her head as though in reply to something she heard, as though she understood everything that she had questioned all her life and felt satisfied in her wisdom. Now that all her prayers were answered, her knowledge complete, her last breath coupled with the still air.

PART III

Pure Sweet Air

Chapter 24

A NORMAL PERSON would have been nervous or more cautious, but Zosia no longer considered herself *normal'na* . . . not anymore. Normalcy belonged to others like the woman sitting across from her, the British journalist who spoke Russian so well. There was only a slight accent to the woman's vowels, and the way she pronounced the telltale soft *l* sounded like a spoiled child's pouty voice. Zosia tried not to notice the accent and to concentrate on making her own voice sound soft and serious on the tape. Still, the woman and her assistants —the ones bustling around with the microphones and tape recorders—were all very kind and sympathetic to her, and Zosia noticed how often they glanced at her with respect for what she had to tell them.

Zosia appreciated the attention but was still somewhat taken aback by the British woman's appearance. Such a different-looking person, her first up close

Westerner. But Zosia knew how much she herself had changed in the nearly three years since the explosion at the Chornobyl plant. She was certainly even dowdier and more disheveled compared with this Westerner. Zosia especially disliked the way her own coarse hair had grown out to reveal too many gray hairs between the dark roots. She'd had neither the time nor money to bother with her hair after their departure from that horrible hospital in Kyiv. How difficult it had been getting out of Ukraine! Mothers and children everywhere— rushing onto the trains, grabbing seats, piling on top of each other, camping out in the aisles where the rude conductors in their blue uniforms yelled at the passengers to get out of their way. Zosia hated the conductors for refusing to sell them tea and sugar wafers. Katia's feelings were hurt by one conductress who ignored her request for a wafer that had fallen off a tray. No one would've gotten anything had Zosia not given in to a fit of frustration and anger. She raised a fuss by grabbing the smug conductress's basket of treats and passing it around to all of the children in their car. "These children are ill!" Zosia shouted, crazed and defiant. "This is the least you can do to help, you *svynia*. Pig!" She threw a handful of kopeks at the conductress, who stumbled away from the frenzied, hungry children. After the ruckus, Zosia half expected to be thrown off the train, and at times during the interminable ride even welcomed the possibility. She and her children had had to sit

in the aisles near the lavatory—an awful place consider-
ing the toilet was nothing more than a hole in the floor
and the door was never properly closed. There was an
overwhelming stench, and rivulets of liquid streamed
out of the toilet directly into Zosia's space.

It had been an agonizingly long train ride with
many, many stops and a six-hour delay because the
tracks were broken. "Too many people on board, that's
why," a woman near Zosia declared to no one in particular. "The train can't carry us all."

Finally, Moscow. Zosia and her children were
almost crushed in the mad rush out of the narrow exits,
and she had to push away several big women who were
suffocating Tarasyk and Katia. "Keep away!" Zosia
shouted at everyone. "Idiots!" She was ready to hit someone. Luckily, she kept her head and her temper until
they were off the train and on the platform.

As quickly as Tarasyk could walk, the three of them
made their way quickly toward the station's vast crowded
lobby. Zosia carried the bags of food and clothes so
Katia had to half pull a listless Tarasyk who more than
once refused to walk and sat down in the middle of the
floor. Finally Katia wouldn't take Tarasyk's hand anymore. "We can't stop now," Zosia said. "Katia, take
Tarasyk over there to that wall. Near Lenin's picture.
Just a few more steps, darlings. Come on, before we get
trampled." Zosia herself nearly fainted and dropped her
bags the moment they reached Lenin's stern gaze. "I

can't get sick," she had told herself. To the children she said calmly, "Now, don't move until I come back."

Zosia had spent another two hours waiting in more long lines to use the phone. She had her cache of kopeks ready in hand in case she had to call more than one friend. She was right. Nobody was expecting her, of course. No one answered. Nearly everyone was at work or standing in a line somewhere else in the city to buy food for the evening's meal. Or at a bar. Typical, Zosia had fumed.

SHE RELATED MOST of this to the British woman whose name was Roberta and who was doing a radio documentary about Chornobyl. Zosia spent most of the day at the woman's borrowed apartment, describing the explosion, the evacuation, the putrid hospital. The foreigner's kind hazel eyes spurred her on, but Zosia still did not trust her enough to fully confess everything. She didn't admit what a coward she felt for deserting Yurko and Marusia like that. Nor did she mention her pregnancy. Inside, Zosia reprimanded herself throughout the interview.

"Where did you stay in Moscow, dear?" the foreigner asked her.

"Wherever I could. With friends. One after another. Then with friends of friends and their relatives," Zosia said. "I tried to register for an apartment in Moscow, but that was impossible. I was put on a waiting list for new housing the government was building for us

Chernobyl workers near Kiev. But I missed an appointment with the housing officials. My son was sick." Zosia bit her tongue so as not to reveal how ill she'd been by then. She had suffered a miscarriage and was so riddled with infections she was convinced that she would be forever sterile—a perfect punishment from God. What a sense of humor He has if He exists, she thought.

Zosia concentrated on the woman's lilac silk scarf. So unusual. She could sell that on the black market in ten seconds and get real German marks or even American dollars for it. She had already sold the embroidered pillow Marusia had given her in Kyiv and the clothes she had gotten from humanitarian aid societies. The only item Zosia refused to sell was the gold necklace of the Virgin, the one Marusia had given her on that last night.

"YES, MARUSIA—IS it?" the journalist said. How very odd it felt to be called by her mother-in-law's old fashioned name. "Marusia, please tell me, what exactly happened to your husband?" Zosia hadn't given the Westerner her real identity. Before, back in the Brezhnev days, anyone could get arrested for even giving lost tourists directions to their hotel. Things had lightened up after Chornobyl, and Gorbachev was allowing a new openness—*glasnost*—after the world had criticized the Soviets for trying to hide the disaster. But Zosia did not trust this "openness" anymore than she did the lying, thieving bureaucrats who kept promising her they would locate her husband, or after slowly poisoning them, give her compensation money and a new home for herself and her children. Why should she trust the same devils who insisted they were doing all they could for her sick son?

Poor Tarasyk. He was so tiny and weak that he could hardly stand up by himself. Even so, not once did he ever complain about the moves from one cramped apartment to another. But during the awful times when he was paralyzed with stomach pains and the pneumonia he endured all the previous winter, his red eyes would well up with tears, and he would look at Zosia as though asking her, "Why?" No more, Zosia vowed. She had to get him out of here. Katia, too. The little girl was also complaining of unusual aches and pains. She had to get her children away. Not even Moscow was safe for them.

THE JOURNALIST OFFERED Zosia a foreign cigarette. Zosia shook her head. She studied the British woman's well-polished fingernails and soft hands. And the wonderfully unusual haircut: a precision cut in the shape of a helmet that flattered the woman's high forehead and long, thin face. When they first met, Zosia had known instantly that Roberta was foreign. Before Roberta had said a word, Zosia guessed she was from the West. The real leather shoes. The simple, well-tailored woolen skirt. The cotton blouse with fancy pearl buttons. The glasses: thin-rimmed, round ones. So different. Nothing like any of it even in the special stores for foreign tourists and high Party officials.

"Tea?" the foreigner asked, smiling at her. Even white teeth. No gold. "No? Now, you were about to tell me about your husband. . . ."

"To get my children out, I had to leave my husband at the hospital in Kiev," Zosia told her. "After my arrival in Moscow, I contacted Kiev, but they told me that he was transferred to a Moscow hospital. Clinic Number Six. It's a special hospital for the Chernobyl victims. He wasn't there. Finally, they told me he died. They gave me some compensation money. And I've gotten a bit more while here, but now the money has been cut off. I can't go back to Kiev either. They won't give me permission anymore. They don't want Chernobyl victims to come back and infect the rest of Kiev."

The journalist bent forward in her chair. "And yourself? How are you doing these days?"

Zosia was disarmed by the woman's concerned face. "I don't know. I'm numb from worrying about everything. Worry will kill me in the end if the radiation doesn't do it first." She'd said too much. She hated to admit she was ill. Her throat itched, she coughed up blood, but she kept it to herself. She believed that if she did otherwise, they'd put her into another worthless hospital and send the children to an orphanage.

The Brit turned off the tape recorder. "Well, I think we have everything we need," she told Zosia. "Thank you so much for your help. The world will know what happened. . . ."

"Yes, the money, please. I need the money *now*," Zosia cut in. "You promised me one hundred rubles if I spoke to you. I took a great risk by doing this. So now, I have to be paid."

The foreigner handed her a business card. "My chief will pay you. Ask for . . ."

"I don't have time. Pay me now. Please!"

The Westerner fumbled in her soft leather brief-case and took out a wallet. "Sorry, I only have English pounds. . . ."

"*Kharasho*—fine. I know where to change them," Zosia said, smiling openly at her for the first time and not caring that Roberta would see how many teeth were missing.

ZOSIA'S ONLY CONCERN the last evening she spent in Moscow was whether she would get her children out of Russia without being arrested for talking to the journalist. She had paid the doctor, the letter was in her purse along with her passport. Her hosts, good friends who had gladly allowed Zosia and the children to stay at their apartment during the past few weeks, were sound asleep in their own room. Tarasyk was also asleep on the divan in the living room. Zosia kissed the knit cap that covered his head, now nearly bald.

She was about to kiss Katia good night when the little girl sat up. "*Mamo*, I can't sleep," Katia said. "We are going away again without *Baba*."

"But darling, we tried to call her in Kyiv lots of

times, and we've written letters to the hospital, and *Baba* doesn't answer," Zosia said.

"Write to our house," Katia said. "Tell her we're going away, but we'll see her someday. So she won't worry."

"Write to the house in the village?" Zosia brightened up and kissed the child's tangled hair. "Good idea! Maybe she's there. You're such a smart girl." Together, she and Katia sat on the parquet floor while Zosia composed a letter which she read to the little girl, who listened as intently as though it were a story:

> *10 September 1989*
> *Dear Mamuniu,*
> *I'm hoping that by some miracle you get this letter—our last before we leave Moscow. We've had a rough time, and Tarasyk is very sick, so we are going to a sanatorium in Georgia.*

Zosia read the next section to herself silently:

> *I contacted the hospital in Kyiv about Yurko. First, they told me he was transferred to Moscow. I searched everywhere and later was told that he's not alive. But there's no official record about his death. So, please tell me what really happened after we left you at the hospital and if he is still alive or not.*

Out loud, Zosia continued:

I know that we never had a phone, but I tried calling the post office in Starylis to send you a message. The lines don't work. So, I want you to please call this number as soon as you can. We are leaving Russia tomorrow but you can talk to my friends Stefan and Tatiana, and tell them where Yurko is and how you are. I will contact my friends when I get to Georgia. And then you can come live with us where it is warm and sunny and healthy!

Katia sends her love. She has headaches and is sick, but not as bad as Tarasyk. Poor boy, he cries to himself and doesn't complain, but he doesn't want to eat, and so all of our attention is on him right now.

Pray for us so that we'll be together again someday, safe and well. I hope that you are alive, and healthy! I am taking a chance sending this to Starylis, but I don't know where else to send it.

Call my friends at 095-032-45-89-21. We kiss you—yours always, Zosia

Mamo, please try to find a phone and tell the operator the number—I know this is hard for you, but after all that we've been through, this really is nothing.

The little girl nodded her approval and insisted on adding her own message:

Babusiu, *don't worry! We will see you*
again! I kiss you every night in my dreams. Yours,
Katia.

Writing the letter wearied Zosia more than her
ordeal with the journalist, more than arguing with doctors and finally bribing them. She tucked Katia in the
divan next to Tarasyk, climbed in with them, and immediately fell asleep.

In her dream, she was back in Starylis. It must have
been a birthday or some occasion, because there were
several people in the kitchen. Yurko and Marusia were
there, younger and laughing and talking with one another. Zosia brought in a cake she made, and she was
laughing along with the others who were joking about
how she had suddenly become such an expert baker. She
was happy and tried to cut the cake, but she was doubled
over with laughter. . . .

She woke up. Startled, Zosia watched the front
door. No one knocked or rang the doorbell. A breeze
wafted through the long gauze draperies, and diesel
buses and taxis rumbled on the street. But that was all.
No one came for her. The sky was gray, but it was daylight. In a few more hours, she and her children would
be on their way. Zosia was giddy and hugged herself to
keep from dancing on the makeshift bed and waking her
innocent children who needed every minute of blissful
sleep.

THE TRIP WAS easy. Her friends' car got them quickly to the airport without the usual stalled motor problems. Zosia and the children got out of the car very near the door to the airport terminal so as not to attract attention from the Red Army soldiers who were randomly detaining lingering travelers and demanding to know where they were going and why.

Once inside the terminal, Zosia was surprised by the almost kindly treatment the soldiers showed her and the children when they checked their passport. One soldier, a young man with acne, carried Tarasyk in his arms to the shuttle bus that would take them to the plane headed for Tbilisi.

At last, the plane roared higher and higher into the smoky clouds, and Zosia felt giddy again. She looked out of the tiny porthole window to catch a final glimpse of diminishing fir trees shrouded in mist. "See, children," she said. "This is how God looks down on the world when He's in heaven." Zosia was surprised to hear herself utter such an odd thing. She knew that no one heard her in the noisy cabin, and she realized it was what Marusia would have said.

Their seats tilted further back as the plane pushed higher into the air. Zosia shut her eyes and felt the plane's engines humming beneath her feet, rocking and vibrating her entire body, pulling them all through gravity— the sick earth's last desperate grab for her soul and her children's souls. She relished her light-headedness and no longer feared anything, not even the radiation. She was a planet spinning out of its orbit, a comet soaring through space, a cloud dissolving into pure sweet air where no one, nothing could touch her.

ACKNOWLEDGMENTS

Great appreciation is due . . .

. . . for the thousand kindnesses of: Shannon Ravenel; Dana Stamey; Nancy Pate; Marta Kolomayets; Ksenia Kiebuzinski, Librarian, Harvard Ukrainian Research Institute; Alex Kuzma, Director of Development for the Children of Chornobyl Relief Fund; the Popowich family of Kyiv; the Pahuta family of Drohobych, Ukraine; Cousin Irina of Lviv; the *Prosvita* students in Ukraine; and the late Henry Sauerwein of the Helene Wurlitzer Foundation.

. . . the sanctuaries where various incarnations of this book were written: the Helene Wurlitzer Foundation of New Mexico, the Dorset Colony, the Edna St. Vincent Millay Colony of the Arts, the Ragdale Foundation, and the Mary Anderson Center for the Arts.

. . . the blessed first readers, faith keepers, and kindred visionaries: Gwyn Hyman Rubio, Ruth Ginsberg-Place, Kathleen Riggs, Terry Bryant, Shelly and Lance Hedstrom, Michael, Mom, and all the Zabytko-Zaraska clan.